KILL OR BE KILLED

Hovik stood very quietly for a while, back pressed against the front wall, eyes closed to concentrate on listening. It didn't take all that long. He heard the man coming up the alley behind the store well before the back door began to ease open. The guy was really trying, too, Hovik thought, as he moved into position by the door, really doing his best to move silently, but he wasn't worth a damn at it.

The rectangle of light from the opening door silhouetted the man for a moment as he stepped inside. Hovik's left arm went around his neck from behind, forearm across the throat, cutting off air before any sound could escape. The big knife in Hovik's right fist came around and disappeared up to the hilt, going in just below the breastbone . . .

"It's tough, it's nasty. I loved it."
—Jim Morris, author of *War Story* and
Devil's Secret Name,
on *Pockets of Resistance*

ALSO BY WILL SUNDOWN

Pockets of Resistance

Published by
POPULAR LIBRARY

ATTENTION: SCHOOLS AND CORPORATIONS

POPULAR LIBRARY books are available at quantity discounts with bulk purchase for educational, business, or sales promotional use. For information, please write to SPECIAL SALES DEPARTMENT, POPULAR LIBRARY, 666 FIFTH AVENUE, NEW YORK, N Y 10103

**ARE THERE POPULAR LIBRARY BOOKS
YOU WANT BUT CANNOT FIND IN YOUR LOCAL STORES?**

You can get any POPULAR LIBRARY title in print. Simply send title and retail price, plus 50¢ per order and 50¢ per copy to cover mailing and handling costs for each book desired. New York State and California residents add applicable sales tax. Enclose check or money order only, no cash please, to POPULAR LIBRARY, P. O. BOX 690, NEW YORK, N Y 10019

THE HELLBOUND TRAIN

WILL SUNDOWN

POPULAR LIBRARY

An Imprint of Warner Books, Inc.

A Time Warner Company

POPULAR LIBRARY EDITION

Copyright © 1991 by William Sanders
All rights reserved.

Popular Library® and the fanciful P design are registered trademarks of Warner Books, Inc.

Cover design by Don Puckey
Cover art by Keith Birdsong

Popular Library books are published by
Warner Books, Inc.
666 Fifth Avenue
New York, N.Y. 10103

 A Time Warner Company

Printed in the United States of America

First Printing: December, 1990

10 9 8 7 6 5 4 3 2 1

**DEDICATED TO
ALL MY FAMILY AND FRIENDS
OF THE KIOWA TRIBE
*AHO***

1

When Mackenzie was done burying his wife he leaned on the shovel for a moment, thinking that there should be something more to do, perhaps some words to say; but there was nothing. A few fragments of long-forgotten ritual passed through his mind—*I am the resurrection and the something, he that believeth in me something something, ashes to ashes, we commit unto the deep the bodies of these our comrades*—but the meaningless words only annoyed him, and, without knowing that he did so, he moved a hand across his face as if to brush them away.

Then he turned and looked back across the sunlit yard at the bodies of the three men who had killed her, and whom he had just killed, and he thought briefly of burying them too, but it was no more than a passing impulse. Let them lie where they had fallen, the two beside the house and the third sprawled in the shade of the trees he had almost reached; Mackenzie would be gone soon enough and there was no one else near enough to care.

He had seen them, and what they were doing, the moment he had stepped out of the woods behind the house. He had killed them immediately, without words or hesitation, with three precise shots from the .22 rifle with which he had been hunting squirrels, the snap snap snap of the little cartridges sounding trivial and childish in the still mountain air. The third one, the one who had almost made it to the cover of the trees, had cried out just before Mackenzie shot him, a single high-pitched shout of anger or fear; that had been the only other sound.

But none of it had been in time to help the woman whose body had already lain lifeless and white in the afternoon sun, her torn and bloody clothing scattered across the early-summer grass, mixed with the wash she had been taking off the line. . . .

He threw the shovel angrily in no particular direction and began walking toward the house. Halfway there he stopped, turned, and looked back at the mound of raw earth under the trees; his mouth opened slightly, but all that came out was a low hoarse sound, almost inaudible, without words. After a second he turned again and continued his walk. He did not look back again.

Inside, he moved purposefully through the little cabin, collecting what he would need. It did not take long. In this isolated place, with the constant possibility of a visit by human predators of one kind or another, he had always made a point of keeping their gear together, ready to take to the woods in a hurry if need be.

His old frame rucksack already held a light down sleeping bag, good enough for the mild nights of the Sierra summer —God knew where he might be by the time the weather turned cool again—and a small camouflage-patterned nylon tarp, as well as a couple of aluminum cookpots and a plastic water bottle. A check of the side pockets turned up the usual odds and ends of trial gear: firemaking kit—including a bottle of carefully hoarded matches, sealed in wax—compass, hooks and fish line, nylon cord, a couple of homemade candles, a small whetstone. There was also a small plastic box containing an assortment of first-aid supplies, though he wondered why he bothered; the meager contents had to be at least ten years old, unlikely to be much good by now.

From the shelves by the back door he took a number of things, putting some into the pack immediately, weighing others in his hand and considering, putting some back or simply tossing them on the floor. Going into the kitchen, he packed a few food items—not much, a small cloth bag of cornmeal and another of dried meat; he would live off what he could find or shoot—and, after a moment's study, he took the big butcher knife and stuck it in his belt.

All this time he moved with the deliberate, almost mechanical efficiency of one who knows that only through absolute concentration and methodical action can he function at all. His face was blank and very pale. Only once did a kind of near-smile flicker across his mouth, when he came across a big flashlight: why the hell had he saved *that*, when there probably wasn't a working flashlight battery left in California, maybe in North America? But the expression never reached his eyes.

Satisfied at last with the pack's contents, he set it down by the door with a soft thump and moved to the little hallway and the gun cabinet.

He had a fair little arsenal, built up over the years mostly by chance; he was no great fancier of firearms, but cartridges were damnably hard to come by in any caliber, so when you happened to acquire a piece with even a few rounds of ammunition, you hung onto it until you'd shot it dry. Most of the weapons in the home-built cabinet were useless now for want of ammunition, in fact, but there was still a fair choice on hand.

He looked them over, took down a few and hefted them and considered: a military M16 assault rifle, an old .30-30 saddle carbine, a scope-sighted .308 Remington, an automatic 12-gauge shotgun. In the end, however, he decided to stay with the little .22 that was already standing by the door. It wasn't a very powerful weapon, but it was light, relatively quiet—important when moving into strange country, where the sound of a shot could bring gangs of looters and bushwhackers and paramilitary goons—and capable of killing anything up to and including smallish deer with careful shooting. Or men; Christ, there was proof enough of that, lying out in the yard . . . and he could carry a large quantity of the tiny cartridges without noticing the weight.

Still, the .22 had almost no stopping power; at close quarters it wouldn't be much help. And the bears had been very numerous lately, and getting entirely too bold and aggressive, their old fear of man fading—no wonder, considering how rare man had become; the bears undoubtedly outnumbered the humans in this part of California by now—and the .22 would only enrage a bear. Mackenzie took down the long-nosed .357 Magnum revolver, still in the leather holster and cartridge belt with the Nevada Highway Patrol markings, and buckled it on.

Finally, after a long ragged sigh, he went into the bedroom. His face was still without expression, but for the first time there was a little hesitation, a seeming uncertainty, in his movements; he walked as if wading in soft sand.

He stood at the battered old dresser, seeing himself in the

big mirror he had taken from a gutted clothing store in a deserted town whose name he could no longer recall. The view was not particularly exceptional: basic white male, middle-aged and, barring a bit of extra bulk in the chest and shoulders, middle-sized. Dark curly hair, cut short and graying heavily at the temples, framed a face that unoriginal journalists had once liked to describe as "craggy." Just now it was a bad face, the skin pulled very tight and something terrible in the pale blue eyes, but he was not really looking.

He fumbled aimlessly through an upper drawer, not sure what he was looking for, except that it seemed he ought to take something, some sort of memento to remember the woman he had just buried, the life they had had here. There was not even a picture of her anywhere in the cabin. When he had found her ten years ago, alone and half mad with hunger in the burned-out ruins of Fresno, she had had nothing but the rags she wore, no purse or wallet with cards and keys and photos—and cameras and photography and darkrooms formed a subject now as forgotten as overpopulation.

The drawer seemed to hold mostly his own junk, anyway, the sort of thing a man puts away and resists domestic pressures to discard: dead pipes, buttons broken off and never sewn back on, a pocketknife with a broken blade, a Marine Corps hat emblem, a single silver oak leaf. His scrabbling fingers found and turned over a bit of stiff fabric the size of his palm, the once-bright colors faded, and he stopped and stared down at it; after a few seconds he picked it up and held it before his face in the poor light, the strange almost-smile pulling at his mouth again.

It was his astronaut's patch.

With an abrupt angry motion he threw the patch back in the drawer and turned away. The hell with it; the hell with all of it. Let it all remain here, just as it was. None of it had anything to do with him any more.

He picked up his pack and shrugged into the straps, feeling the familiar weight settle into place. Rifle in his left hand, he opened the door and went down the steps, leaving the door open behind him, and down the trail toward the distant road.

The old man at the store in the village said, "Look. I got some more papers a couple of days back."

It wasn't really a store, not any more, though it had been one a decade ago; it was just a dark, bad-smelling place where a crazy old man did a little trading in this and that and pored over the stacks of old newspapers and magazines that he called his "archive." For that matter the village wasn't really a village, just a collection of falling-down houses where a couple of families still managed to exist. It was a place Mackenzie had rarely gone, over the last few years; he wished now that he had not come today, but it was too late.

The old man said, "Look," again. He was spreading newspapers on the counter, fanning them to show the yellow cracking front pages. "Just look at these headlines. History." He began reading aloud. " 'Epidemic in Western States. Virus Spreads Nationwide, State of Emergency Declared. Administration Declares Martial Law. Rioting in Major Cities.' Shows you how far the gover'ment had lost control," he put in, grinning gummily at Mackenzie. "Way they were running things back before the Plague, they'd never have allowed a newspaper to print anything like that." He chuckled wheezily, turning papers. "Notice how the papers change, though, over the next month or so—shorter and shorter, sloppy-looking layouts, lots of typos, and hardly any pictures. News gets more and more local, too—people putting them out couldn't find out what was going on in the next county, let alone overseas. Can't figure why they stuck to their jobs, ever'body else running wild trying to get out of the cities, trying to survive."

He held up a single tabloid-size page, bearing only an off-center logo, a single headline, and a few columns of ragged type. The headline had been composed by someone with a degree of gallows humor; it read simply:

THE END

"Know what this is?" the old man crowed. "Very last edition, ever, of the San Francisco *Chronicle*. Best I can tell, they had just a little handful of people left in the place—maybe half a dozen, probably all of them sick with the Plague or one of the other bugs that were going around the cities by then—and they put this thing out just as a kind of last gesture, I guess." He shook his head. "I traded a whole box of twelve-gauge shells for this. Would of given two if he'd held out."

Mackenzie wondered how much longer it was going to be before some passing drifter killed the old man. From outside, however, came the yaps of the pack of pit bulls that had kept anyone from doing it so far.

Mackenzie said, "Have you got any maps?"

"Maps." The old man put the paper down reluctantly and peered at Mackenzie. "Road maps?"

"I've got a California road map already. Don't you have any, you know, contour maps, Geological Survey quads, anything like that?" He knew it was a long shot; still, the old man's pack-rat compulsions might extend to maps as well.

But the old man was shaking his head. "Don't know a

thing about that sort of business. Course I've got my own maps, over on the wall there." He pointed to a number of tacked-up maps of the United States, apparently cut from schoolbooks, their surfaces dotted by colored pins. "Charting the spread of the Plague, the riots, the overall breakdown of, uh, things." He gestured proudly. "But they wouldn't do you any good even if I was to let them go."

He looked at Mackenzie's pack, the rifle, the revolver on his belt. "Taking to the road? Trouble with the Missus?" He cackled. "Need anything else? Got some twenty-two cotterges, good shape."

There were several things Mackenzie needed, and he could have used the .22's, but suddenly he could no longer stand it: the airless room, the yellowing papers, and the old man sitting amid the records of the dead and more-than-dead past. He picked up his rifle from the counter. "You're a ghoul," he said to the old man. "Anybody ever tell you you're a ghoul?"

The wrinkled skinny face went red. Mackenzie realized for the first time that the old man even looked like a vulture. "No call to talk like that," he shrilled as Mackenzie went out the door. "No call at all. This is *history*," he screamed, but Mackenzie was already gone.

It was well into the afternoon by the time Mackenzie left the village, and he made, he guessed, no more than seven or eight miles, walking steadily but without particular haste along the shoulder of the cracked and buckled old blacktop road that led roughly southwest toward the central valleys. He had no particular reason to want to leave the Sierras, and indeed he might change directions before he reached the lower country; it was simply the direction he happened to take. For now he was drifting, having no purpose and feeling no need for one; he felt as weightless as he had ever felt in space.

A rabbit gave him a clear easy shot, late in the afternoon, and he aimed and paused and lowered the rifle, realizing he had no desire to fire it again today. Instead he dug out a strip of jerky—elk, dried last fall in his own backyard—and chewed slowly as he walked along, not really hungry anyway.

Late in the day, as the falling sun lengthened the shadows across the road, he found a clear level spot next to a little creek, out of sight of the road and screened by a stand of tall trees. He laid the sleeping bag on the soft pine needles and stretched out, not bothering with the tarp; the sky was cloudless and the air smelled dry. He built no fire; there was no need.

He lay on his back, head propped on his pack, and watched the woods and then the sky grow dark, and now at last the pain and the loss and the loneliness came surging up through the emptiness inside him and rushed over him like a great black cataract; his eyes closed tight and his fists clenched in a convulsive spasm and then opened and rose to press shaking palms against his face. He did not weep, exactly; only a few tears escaped at the corners of his eyes, and again he made that strange low hoarse sound, though he did not realize he was doing it.

Finally, late into the night, the shaking stopped; his face and body relaxed, in a series of twitches and shudders, and his breathing became more regular. And at last Ross Mackenzie, who had once walked on the Moon, slept.

2

In the next few days Mackenzie walked a great many miles, hiking from first to last light, covering more and more ground as his feet toughened and his legs grew stronger—though he had already been in excellent condition; nothing like the incredible fitness of an astronaut in training, of course, probably there had never been anything quite like that in the history of the world, but he had kept in shape over the years and a decade of hard survival work had burned off any softness.

The long miles represented nothing more than a driven restlessness, not a desire to reach any particular goal. He was still drifting with little sense of direction, occasionally consulting the old Exxon road map when he came to a crossroads or fork, but just as often merely taking whichever turn took his fancy. He followed a series of back roads and the occasional grown-over logging track or fire road, avoiding the main highways where a few bandit gangs and paramilitary bands still cruised—God knew where they got the gas—and he used the map chiefly to avoid towns big enough to be dangerous.

(Sitting one day on a rusting mountain-curve guardrail, chewing the remains of last evening's quail and studying the network of red and blue and yellow lines, he was struck suddenly by a minor irony: gasoline rationing, a deteriorating highway-and-bridge system, and ever-tightening restrictions on personal travel by a paranoid police-state government, had made long-distance private motoring a difficult and uncommon thing for most Americans, years and years before the Plague and the breakdown of an already deteriorating civilization. And yet they had gone on printing and distributing road maps, just as if families still drove off cross-country on holidays to visit Grandma in California! An aphorism popped into his mind, though he did not know if he had heard it somewhere or made it up himself: *It's not over until the illusions are over*.)

At first he continued to work his way down out of the mountains, but as he began to get into the foothills that bordered the great central valleys, he swung more southward, keeping to higher ground. The plains country between the Sierras and the Coast Range was a bad place for a man on foot; there was little game—except for the expanding herds of wild cattle, too big for his light rifle—and the people, such as there were, tended to shoot at strangers on sight, having memories of the first terrible times after the Plague when refugees from the dying cities had swarmed over the farm country looking for food. . . . So it had been the last time Mackenzie had been there, and things were unlikely to have gotten any better. Few things did, nowadays.

He had no trouble getting food; the game was plentiful in the woods and he could have killed far more than he could eat if he had felt the urge. The weather stayed fine; he slept under the stars each night. He met no living people; but one day he came upon a white station wagon beside the road, its doors and windows shut and, in the front seat, the bodies of two adults and a child. The bodies were not much more than skeletons by now, but in the driver's hand was a small pistol.

Now and then Mackenzie passed through little deserted towns, the empty houses and stores and gas stations sometimes burned out, sometimes defaced with painted graffiti and smashed windows, often simply sitting quiet and dark as if the residents had gone away for the weekend. Some of the abandonment, he knew, went back well before the Plague. The nation had already been in the grip of a long economic and social down-spiral, and small rural communities had died off as the people crowded into the overloaded cities in search of work and services. Which, of course, had done a great deal to help the virus take out something like three-quarters of the population inside a year, and the survivors to find other ways to die in the burning streets or on the choked exit roads. Even the vaccine that had appeared in some areas had probably done little good; the distribution system had already broken down and he guessed that for every person saved by the vaccine, one or more had died in the riots at the immunization centers. . . .

He stayed clear of the vacant structures. But on the ninth day, when the sky clouded over and began to dump a cold gray drizzle on the road, he saw a large white house outside a small town and was tempted. Huddling all day and night under a small tarp was unappealing, as was slogging along in the rain, and the place did look thoroughly deserted, weeds and brush high in the yard, a fallen limb lying across the porch.

A quick but thorough reconnaissance turned up no occupants; the boards of the front porch were rotting and risky, but he went around to the rear and found a small door that opened into the garage. It was locked, but a couple of hard kicks smashed it open.

The interior of the garage was dark, but after some straining he got the big main door halfway up on its rusty tracks, enough to let in the gray rainy-day light. There was no car or other motor vehicle in the garage, but on the walls, hung from metal hooks, Mackenzie saw the spindly shapes of several bicycles.

A wonder, he thought, that this place hadn't been found and looted by now. Bicycles were things of great value now gas was almost unobtainable; people had been killed over possession of a rusty old Schwinn or even a set of fresh tires. And these were obviously expensive, sophisticated machines; the owner of the house must have been a real enthusiast—there was even a box of old bicycling magazines in one corner, with fit-looking people in rather silly outfits posing on the covers. Mackenzie studied the bikes, an idea beginning to form in his mind.

The rain went on all day and night; Mackenzie took his time. The lightweight racing machines were too flimsy for his purposes, but there was a sturdy-looking bike with flat handlebars and big tires and built-on luggage racks, the type he believed had been called a "mountain bike." A search of the garage turned up a set of capacious nylon saddlebags and a pouch for the handlebars, as well as tools, spare parts, and a supply of tires and tubes. Mackenzie oiled the chain and sprockets from a brass squirt-can, fitted new rubber to the wheels—the tires and tubes on the bicycle seemed perfectly good, but it was raining and he had nothing better to do—and raised the seat and handlebars to a reasonably comfortable fit. His gear went easily into the large saddlebags; he lashed the rifle across the luggage rack with a couple of rubber bungee cords and put the revolver in the handlebar bag for quick access. In the morning, after a night on the garage floor—he had not ventured into the house itself—he rolled the bicycle down to the highway and swung his leg over, and kicked gingerly off.

He had not ridden a bicycle in years, though he had been a fairly enthusiastic cyclist in his youth; popular myth to the contrary, it took some time to recover the skills, and he wobbled a great deal at first and fell down a couple of times on turns. But gradually it all came back to him, and soon he was spinning down the long grades with a feeling of childish exhilaration, enjoying the speed—it was, he realized, the fastest he had moved in years—and the wind in his face, and refusing to think about the rapidly accumulating pain where his backside contacted the hard narrow little saddle.

The bicycle changed the whole nature of his journey. Before, twenty miles had represented a good day's travel; now, that was no more than a couple of take-it-easy hours. He could do some serious moving if he wanted; he could reach the coast, if nothing stopped him, or the desert country to the south, or even turn east and see how far he could get across the continent. Climbing the steep hills was hard work, but no worse than doing it on foot, and going down the other side was sheer joy. Now and then a fallen tree or a spring-thaw washout blocked the road, and once he had to wade a creek, carrying the bike over his shoulder, where a small bridge had collapsed; but it was easy carrying the light machine over or around obstacles, and it gave his behind a brief rest.

By the end of the second week he was much farther from

his starting point than he had ever considered possible; in fact he was no longer entirely certain just where he was. Somewhere between the high Sierras and the southern end of the San Joaquin Valley, presumably; which narrowed it down to an area only slightly larger than some eastern states, but then he was not really interested in determining his precise location. A couple of times, the last day, he crossed a double set of railroad tracks which seemed to be on roughly the same north-south course as the road. Obviously some sort of main line, judging by the heaviness of the rail stock; Southern Pacific, perhaps? He had no idea; his map did not show railroads.

By this time he no longer had trouble getting to sleep, or awoke shaking and sweating in the middle of the night, and the dreams had begun to leave him alone. When he thought back on the recent past, which was rare, it was as if it had all happened to someone else, something he had read about in a half-forgotten book, vividly written but with no relationship to reality. . . .

Midafternoon, the day it happened: a hot still day, the sun painfully bright in a cloudless sky. Toiling up a steep hill, standing on the pedals, Mackenzie blinked repeatedly as the sweat stung his eyes, and reflected that he ought to stop in the next town and see if he could find some sort of hat. Or a pair of sunglasses; the road here was concrete and the glare off the white surface was blinding. His head was starting to hurt.

Cresting the hill, he shifted into top gear and crouched slightly as the bicycle began to pick up speed on a long curving downhill. The wind in his ears and the whirring swish of the wheels should have been soothing, but today he felt inexplicably edgy and the sounds only annoyed him in a vague dull way. There seemed to be another sound, a distant muted throbbing, very low in pitch but somehow penetrating; he paid it no real mind at first, except to wonder if it might be a fast river. He needed fresh water.

Coasting, rubbing his eyes, he freewheeled across a narrow bridge and through a grove of low-overhanging trees and suddenly found himself whizzing past houses, bumping over cracked and weed-grown street pavement, dodging a pothole beneath the dead gaze of a still-hanging traffic light. A sign said: SPEED LIMIT 25 MPH   CHECKED BY RADAR. Christ, he'd ridden into a town without even knowing it. And, he saw immediately, a town that was far from deserted; several of the houses were obviously occupied, the yards freshly tended, even a few flowers growing in little beds. He saw several flourishing gardens and what looked like a chicken yard. A dog barked at him from the end of a long chain; somebody was feeding that dog, and keeping the area clear of the packs of feral dogs that roamed most of the uninhabited towns. A roughly lettered sign in one yard read FRESH VEGETABLES—WILL TRADE.

Mackenzie braked the bicycle, looking rapidly around, his pulse racing. No people in sight at the moment, nothing moving except the dog. He flipped the handlebar bag open and made sure the .357 was clear for a fast grab. People in these little communities, for all their efforts to maintain some level of "civilization," could be insanely hostile toward outsiders—especially lone outsiders with no apparent purpose to their arrival.

But as he pedaled slowly on up the street, there were still no people to be seen, nor did he have any feeling of being watched from the blank windows of the houses on either side. It was somehow a more disturbing thing than passing through the ghost towns; the hair on the back of his neck was prickling like a wolf's. The low throbbing sound was louder now, too; it almost seemed he could feel a vibration through the ground, coming up through his wheels.

He stood on the pedals and accelerated, wanting now only to get out of this weird place. But then he crested a little hill and came upon a kind of open park or town square, where a number of people stood in a tight-packed group, their backs to him. From somewhere a voice was shouting unintelligibly, sounding angry.

The shock stopped his mind for a moment. It was not a large crowd—perhaps twenty or thirty at most—but it was more people than he had seen at one time in years. As the bicycle rolled to a stop, he saw now that there were other people standing about the square, men in camouflage clothing, holding weapons. Some of them seemed to be pointing their guns at the people in the center of the square. A man in some sort of uniform was standing on a bench, gesturing; he seemed to be the one doing the shouting.

Mackenzie's reactions took over at last. He stood on the pedals, sprinting like a track racer for the nearest side street, hearing voices raised behind him in surprise and then anger. Somewhere an automatic weapon went off in a long burst, bullets snapping hungrily overhead and whining off the pavement nearby.

He shifted up and pedaled harder, wishing for the first time that he had taken one of the racing bikes. Hanging a violent right, he got a brick church between himself and the square, jammed hard up an alley and across a yard, and headed back in what he hoped was the way he had come. If he could get clear of the town he could ditch the bike and lose them in the hills. . . .

He almost made it. Later, he sometimes thought that he might have pulled it off if he had been thirty, even twenty years younger. It was sheer bad luck, though, that the six-man search party happened to come up the side road just as he crossed the bridge; worse luck that they had wit enough to react instantly, spreading out to block his way, and worse yet that the nearest soldier was clever enough to thrust the barrel of his rifle into the spokes of the front wheel, sending Mackenzie flying through the air to land with a graceless sliding thud at their feet. By the time he raised his head, half stunned, there were five M16's pointed at him from less than two meters' distance.

A short red-haired man, wearing three black stripes painted on the sleeves of his camouflage shirt, grinned down at Mackenzie. "Hold on there, hoss," he said cheerfully. "Don't run off so fast. General Decker don't like people who shirk their patriotic duty. Might give him the idea you're some kind of a Comm-you-nist."

One of the men bent over the fallen bicycle. "Anything good?" the red-haired Sergeant said. "Get the bicycle, anyway, we can always use that."

"Couple of guns," the man said, straightening, handing the Sergeant the .22 and the .357.

"Little piss-ant twenty-two? That ain't no gun for a grown man. Hey, nice short gun, though." The redhead admired the Magnum briefly before tucking it into his belt, pulling down his camouflage shirt to cover it. "Always wanted me one of these."

Someone said, "You think you'll get to keep it, Red?"

"I will," Red said pointedly, "if certain people keep their mouths shut. Certain people might like to remember they would just as well not get on the bad side of people who ever now and then get to pick details for certain jobs. If you know what I mean and I think you do."

He watched as Mackenzie got to his feet. "You ain't about to be a pain in the ass, are you? I mean, you try to resist or run or give us any shit, we'll just naturally have to stomp your old ass some. Okay?"

Mackenzie nodded. He could not speak; he had been out of breath even before the fall knocked the remaining bits of air out of him. His heart seemed to be about to break a hole in his ribs.

"Good," the Sergeant said. "So now you pick up the bicycle and walk ahead of us, pushing it. You even look like swinging a leg over it, we'll shoot your old ass off."

They marched him back to the square. The armed men there, he saw, had now formed the people up into a rough column and were herding them toward a side street. "Leave the wheel," Red said, "and go join the parade."

Mackenzie joined the group, glad to lose his dangerous individuality for the moment. There were men and women, he saw, in roughly equal numbers; there seemed to be no children or really old people. A tall man in faded overalls stepped out of line and began to speak, waving his hands angrily; as Mackenzie watched, several M16 buttplates slammed into the small of his back and he screamed and fell, while shiny black boots kicked at him. "Next one gets shot," someone shouted. "Now move it, God damn it."

Mackenzie saw now that there were other people across the street, watching: old people, they appeared to be, skinny and hunched, no more than half a dozen of them, and, clinging to their hands, a number of children of varying sizes. A couple of men with rifles covered them. None of them made any sound, except the low whines of the smaller children.

The column of prisoners moved down the street, which sloped steeply downhill. The townspeople seemed to know where they were going. The throbbing rumble in his ears was now very loud and he wondered if he had hit his head when he fell.

But then the street opened onto a broad open lot, overgrown with tall weeds and strewn with litter, and Mackenzie saw that they had come to the railroad tracks. And saw, too, something that was not merely incredible but altogether impossible.

Sitting on the track directly ahead, looking bigger than the whole world, were a pair of big diesel locomotives, wisps of bluish smoke drifting upward from their exhausts. The ground shook with the rumble of their idling engines. The flat side of the lead engine bore a huge painted representation of the flag of the United States. The second locomotive was decorated with an equally enormous painting of an angry-looking bald eagle, its wings outspread.

Behind the engines, stretching back along the tracks, were the cars of a strange-looking train. Mackenzie could see only the first few cars from where he stood, but the second car back was a flatcar that bore a dark-green heavy tank. The turret was traversed through ninety degrees, the big gun aimed over their heads in the general direction of the town. A man stood in the turret hatch, a black beret on one side of his head, leaning on a machine gun.

The men in camouflage were driving their prisoners on, using rifle butts and boot-toes freely. Mackenzie stayed in the middle of the group and kept his head down; he could see only that they were passing along next to the train. At last the column jerked to a stop and then began moving unevenly forward again as the guards herded them toward the open doors of a rusty boxcar. Mackenzie saw a faded Indian sun symbol and the barely legible words SANTA FE.

Some of the women and the shorter men had to be helped aboard by the others. Mackenzie hoisted himself up when his time came and scrambled to his feet, picking a place against the steel wall, next to the door. There seemed to be plenty of room, however.

"Ladies and gents," someone shouted from outside. "Assholes one and all. Welcome to the Army of America."

3

A burst of automatic gunfire laced across the street and chewed divots out of the already riddled front of the hardware store. Inside, Frank Hovik ducked and cursed as bullets came through the window and shards of the remaining glass rained down around him.

"Jesus *Christ*," he said, more in exasperation than anything else.

Raising his head slowly and cautiously, he peered over the windowsill at the building across the street, which appeared to have been, for God's sake, a barber shop. The windows were smashed there too, but he could see nothing of the interior. He considered firing a few rounds just to make them keep their heads down, but he did not have all that much ammunition on him. Let the silly bastards waste their own cartridges, if it got them off; the way they'd been shooting, they must own a bullet factory. Three of them against one lone man, and here they'd fired enough rounds to take out a platoon and still hadn't hit him! Unless you counted the bleeding cut on his left shoulder, just above the tattoos of the winged skull and the Harley-Davidson emblem, and that was from a piece of flying glass.

Three of them: actually four, to begin with, but that hadn't lasted long enough to count. The fourth one lay in the middle of the street, arms outspread, staring up at the California sky but almost certainly not seeing it. Hovik had killed him in the first few seconds of the fight, two thirty-caliber soft-nosed slugs through the chest, twice as many as necessary but Hovik had been in a hurry.

Moving slowly, keeping solid brick and plaster between himself and the street, Hovik got to his feet. Something in the sound of that last burst of fire was eating at him.

He was a big, heavy-muscled man, not particularly tall, but wide across the shoulders, with the bull neck of a wrestler. Long ago a prison guard had said that Hovik was built like the biggest God-damned fire hydrant you ever saw; it was still an apt description, though at age fifty he had begun to carry a little bit of padding here and there.

A bristling black beard, heavily streaked with gray, covered most of his face, but what showed through was not all that reassuring; the windburned skin was lined and wrinkled as an old set of motorcycle leathers, and a long scar crossed his forehead. His coarse black hair, which was also going gray, was almost shoulder-length, held in place by a red bandanna headband—for which he had already kicked himself mentally; it might look sharp around home but it was a suicidally silly thing to wear on a foraging run into a strange town, where it was always possible to find yourself being shot at.

Still, he mused as he squinted one-eyed around the window frame, this situation didn't make any kind of sense. Why the hell were they after him at all?

It had begun as a purely accidental encounter; Hovik had come around a corner and there they had been, coming up the middle of the main street, weapons in their hands, one of them apparently giving another a light. Before he could duck back out of sight, they had reacted instantly and mindlessly, shouting and yip-yapping like excited dogs, opening fire without so much as a challenge—or, fortunately, taking careful aim. There were no challenges or warning shots, and they were clearly trying to kill him, not just scare him away; only their bad marksmanship had allowed him to reach the cover of the hardware store. From which he had drilled the nearest one, causing the others to hole up across the street, and there they had all been, pretty much all morning.

None of it, he thought, made any sense at all; what were they after? He had nothing of any value on him, beyond his rifle and the .45 automatic on his belt, and they certainly had plenty of guns of their own; they had already fired off more ammunition than they could hope to get off his body if they got him. True, he had come down from the hills on a motorcycle that was worth quite a bit, maybe worth killing for —others had tried, from time to time—but it was hidden in the woods outside of town, and even if they had found it there was nothing to stop them from simply riding or pushing it away without bothering with all this OK Corral nonsense.

Stupid, Hovik concluded, just plain numb-nuts stupid. Which was unusual; most of the looters and bushwhackers who haunted the abandoned towns had at least a certain level of ratlike smarts, even though they might be barely human in other ways. In fact there weren't many really stupid people left anywhere anymore; there had been too many years in which it took some degree of intelligence just to survive, and the authentic dummies had been pretty well weeded out. . . .

True, there was *going* to be one hell of a problem along those lines one of these years, because some of the smaller groups of survivors were working hard at getting dangerously inbred—some of those isolated settlements, you had brothers fucking sisters and fathers fucking daughters and the old street insult was just a simple statement of fact—but the results weren't old enough to shoot anybody, yet.

These clowns were pretty young, though, from the brief look he'd gotten, and the skinny, ragged body in the street didn't appear to have been making out all that well. Maybe, Hovik thought, they were crazy. That was something you did see, and it wasn't all that rare.

He knew now what he'd heard, or thought he'd heard. It shouldn't be hard to check.

He worked the red headband off and hung it on the end of his rifle barrel. This one, he thought, was so God-damned old these punks probably hadn't even heard of it. He unholstered his .45 and fired a shot at random out the window, just to get their attention, and then he stuck the rifle muzzle past the window frame a little way and jiggled the red bandanna up and down.

The shots came immediately, and he pulled the rifle back and nodded to himself. Only two guns firing over there: some kind of military automatic, probably an M16, and a little pistol-caliber chopper like an Uzi or an Ingram. Where the hell were they getting ammunition to feed those things?

And, of course, where the hell was the third man?

Hovik stood very quietly for awhile, back pressed against the front wall, eyes closed to concentrate on listening. It didn't take all that long. He heard the man coming up the alley behind the store well before the back door began to ease open. The guy was really trying, too, Hovik thought as he moved into position by the door, really doing his best to move silently, but he just wasn't worth a damn at it.

The rectangle of light from the opening door silhouetted the man for a moment as he stepped inside. Hovik's left arm went around his neck from behind, forearm across the throat, cutting off air before any sound could escape. The big knife in Hovik's right fist came around and disappeared up to the hilt, going in just below the breastbone, angling upward to pierce the heart. The man's body convulsed violently; his feet came clear off the floor for a moment as Hovik held him up, and then he went limp. A sudden rank smell drifted up to Hovik's nose as the dead man filled his pants.

Hovik let the body to the floor, taking the weapon from the limp fingers. A sawed-off pump shotgun, twelve-gauge by the feel of it, not a bad choice for a job like this. A search of the body turned up a few shells and a snub-nosed revolver, its trigger guard hacksawed away, guaranteeing that the owner would have shot himself with it sooner or later.

He could not, Hovik decided, have been more than eighteen years old. If that. Hovik sighed, shook his head, and thought of something.

The kid was nowhere near Hovik's size or build, but he did have fairly long dark hair, and he wore a black sleeveless shirt that might, at a distance and for a moment, look vaguely like Hovik's black tee-shirt. Anyway, Hovik didn't think the people across the street had ever gotten a good look at him. And then, too, he was dealing with a couple of nervous morons.

The kid was skinny, no problem to drag to the front of the store. Hovik put the red bandanna around the corpse's head and held him more or less upright with one arm. "Show time," he said under his breath.

The sawed-off shotgun made a deafening blast inside the low-ceilinged store. Hovik jacked the action clumsily and fired again into the floor, just for general effect; then, letting out a loud scream, he threw the dead body through the smashed window.

The corpse's clothing caught on the remaining bits of glass, making the upper half of the body pitch realistically out the window, arms flopping, head dangling. Hovik fired the shotgun once more into the body, making it jerk horribly, and waited.

The reaction across the street actually took longer than he had expected, say about three seconds. Then a high excited voice called, "Don? You get him, Don?" Another voice rose in a wild hysterical yell that ended in a weird laugh.

The kid with the M16 came out first, the other one following hesitantly after a brief wait. Hovik let the first one get clear to the middle of the street, the other one just stepping off the sidewalk, and then he put the shotgun to his shoulder and aimed as best he could with no sights and fired. The buckshot knocked the kid back, dropping him within a few feet of the body that already lay there. The flat boom of the shotgun racketed briefly down the street, echoing off the fronts of buildings.

Hovik racked the action and pointed at the last bushwhacker, who was starting to whirl as if to run, but when he pulled there was only a click. Cursing, he threw the empty shotgun away—served him right for depending on an idiot to keep his piece loaded all the way—and reached for his rifle.

The surviving bushwhacker was halfway up the street by now, running hard. He seemed to have thrown down his machine pistol, probably to run faster. He was making no attempt to take cover. His torn shirt fluttered behind him as he ran.

Hovik covered him with the sights and stopped. Why shoot him now he was hauling ass? But Hovik was alone and many miles from home, and it was always possible the silly son of a bitch might get his nerve back and pull something.

Hovik sighed again, laid the sights once more on the center of the rapidly retreating back, and squeezed.

When the distant figure had stopped moving, Hovik slung his rifle over his shoulder and began to walk back toward where he had left his motorcycle. But then he stopped, shook his head, and turned back toward the row of silent storefronts. As much shit as he'd had to go through here, he thought sourly, might as well see if he could get something out of the place. If nothing else he ought to get the guns off the bodies, though he guessed they'd be dirty and rusty as hell, and a wonder if they had more than a few cartridges left.

At the door of the hardware store he stopped and looked back, up and down the street. A growing drone told him the flies were already starting to swarm.

"Shit," he said tiredly, and turned and went inside.

It was late afternoon when Hovik finally rode up the winding gravel road and through the big gate at the top of the hill, waving a left-handed greeting to the teenage boy sitting up in the wooden guard tower. Have to stop that business, he thought, big healthy kid like that getting to spend the day sitting up there playing with himself; whatever risk of attack there might be these days, it didn't justify wasting that much of the work force. Anyway, no serious attacker was going to come marching up the road in broad daylight and try to enter through the main gate; and if any drifters or bushwhackers turned up at the hilltop camp, the packs of half-wild dogs that roamed the area would bark a warning.

He eased the motorcycle to a stop in front of a large low-roofed log house and toed it into neutral and shut off the engine. Kicking the sidestand down, he climbed off and gave the bike a long look and a slow headshake. A lifelong Harley-Davidson loyalist, he was still more than a little embarrassed to find himself riding a Japanese-made machine. But sometimes you had to be practical; getting around these parts involved riding a lot of washed-out dirt back roads, and the blacktop wasn't much better nowadays. A dirt bike was much more useful for that kind of riding, besides being more maneuverable in the close quarters of a town, and Harley had never made anything along those lines.

He had a Harley—actually two, but only one was in working order—that he kept in a nearby shed, but he seldom got to ride it except on the rare long-distance highway run. The way the highways were going, he might not be doing even that much longer; last spring some of them had gone down to the old Interstate and tried to go south to Sacramento, only to find that slides had cut the freeway in several places and some of the bridges had collapsed in the last earthquake. They'd given up and come home after less than a hundred miles.

This bike was a 600cc. Honda, and he had to admit it was pretty decent for what it was. The engine was nice and simple, anyway, and reliable as a ball bat: just one great big piston thumping up and down and making enough torque to damn near ride up the side of a house. It used a lot less gas than a Harley, too. Probably he ought to go to something smaller, like a 250, and save even more gas, but hell, a man had to have *some* standards.

He started to go toward the big log house, but then a familiar figure came out of the house across the drive and strode toward him, calling out a greeting. "Joe Jack," Hovik said. "Got some stuff here."

Joe Jack Mad Bull, short and dark and very Cheyenne, split his face in a white-toothed grin as he came around the parked Honda. "Starting to worry about you, bro," he said. Long black braids danced against his bare chest as he shook his head. "Judith's been getting real edgy, last couple hours. Wherever you been, I hope you brought her back something good. She's got that massacree look on, you know?"

Hovik unhooked the bungee lashings on the Honda's luggage rack and began handing guns to Joe Jack, whose eyes were beginning to get larger. "Probably need cleaning," he said, passing over the two M16's and then the Ingram. "One of the sixteens is so rusty and fucked-up it's probably only good for parts, but then we can always use that kind of stuff. Guy that had it never got off a shot, so there ought to be at least a few rounds in the clip anyway."

He held out a large red shoulder bag, a purse taken from the discount clothing store next to the shot-up barber shop. "Got some ammo in there, couple of pistols—pieces of shit, but they might do for trade goods."

The Cheyenne was looking distinctly shaken by now. "Jesus," he said, staring down at the guns in his arms. Then, seeing the cut on Hovik's arm, "Hey, what the hell you been *doing*, man? Where you been? You get into a fight?"

Hovik shrugged, lifting the nylon duffel bag from behind the Honda's seat. "Ran into some bushwhackers in that town down the valley—what's the name of that place? The one, you know, Billy Blackhorse got jumped by that pack of wild dogs last year." He hefted the clanking duffel bag. "Speaking of Billy, you see him, tell him to come over. I got some stuff in here he wanted."

"Jesus," Joe Jack Mad Bull said again. "Three guns, so you must—nah, I'm not asking. You hear? I'm not asking."

"Yeah, well, there was a shotgun too, but we got plenty of them already. Hell, we got more guns around this place right now than we'll ever have people to use. Trade half of them right now for a six-pack of cold Bud. Look," he said as Joe Jack started to speak, "I'll tell you all about it tomorrow, okay? It's been a hell of a long day."

They stood in silence for a moment. Joe Jack looked up and down the long gravel drive, at the row of log houses and sheds, the goats drifting along the fence line and the mixed pack of dogs and small children doing something suspicious-looking down by the wellhouse. "Damn," he said to Hovik, "to think this place used to be a Boy Scout camp." He looked down at the guns. "Sure as hell ain't any Boy Scouts around here now, are there?"

"Yeah," Hovik agreed, "but you could say we try to be prepared."

From inside the house behind him a woman's voice called, "Hovik? Hovik, is that you?"

Hovik said, "Oh, shit."

"Long day, huh?" Joe Jack said. "Tell you what, old horse, I think it's about to get a lot longer. . . ."

Judith said, "You *what*?"

Hovik took off one lug-soled boot and wiggled his toes. "Christ," he said, "I told you, it wasn't any big deal. There weren't but four of them and they didn't know shit. Your grandma could have taken them."

"And I suppose God came down, before you went into

that town, and handed you a notarized guarantee you wouldn't run into anything you couldn't handle?" She wrinkled her nose as he took off his other boot. "My God, give me those socks. Dammit, Hovik, as many times as you've told Joe Jack and the others about going foraging alone in those places—"

"Okay, okay, it was a jackoff thing to do. The four bushwhackers weren't the only stupid assholes in that town today, right? I admit it." He leaned back on the butt-sprung old couch and closed his eyes briefly. "You're right. Now let up on me, will you?"

She stood close to him and reached out to touch his shoulder next to the cut. "Looks as if you got tagged a little," she said more quietly.

"Ah, hell, you've done worse with your fingernails on a hot night." He opened his eyes and leered up at her. "Not *lately*, of course, but we could do something about that—"

"Tie a knot in it," she said, not quite managing to keep a grin from pulling at the corners of her mouth. "Wait, I'll clean that up. God knows what sort of germs there are in a place like that."

She moved across the room and bent to open a big wooden chest. Hovik watched appreciatively. She was a medium-sized woman in her late thirties with thick black hair done up in a single long braid down her back. Just now she wore a thin loose khaki shirt and blue running shorts that showed off her fine tanned legs; she had big solid breasts and if she was a little on the wide side across the bottom, maybe getting a little wider in the last few years, that was fine too because that was the way Hovik liked it. He said, "You sure you're not part Czech, woman? For a Jew you sure got a Czech ass on you."

She straightened, holding a small bottle and a clean white cloth, and came back toward him. "My old man, always a gentleman of refinement. Hold still."

The home-distilled alcohol burned as she swabbed the cut. "So we finally found some use for Billy's white lightning," he remarked. "Let's see, so far he's made stuff to kill germs with, run a truck engine, and start fires. I wish to Christ he'd manage to make something you can stand to drink."

"Seems to me I've seen you swallow your share."

"Yeah, but it's not something I take *pride* in." He watched her put the alcohol bottle away. "Well, anyway, I was going to say—"

There was a knock on the door. Hovik yelled, "Come in," and a tall, thin, homely young man with long loose black hair entered and said, "Joe Jack said you got the stuff we need."

"Oh, yeah, right." Hovik got up and handed over the duffel bag. "It's in there, what there is of it."

Billy Blackhorse started to unzip the bag but Hovik said, "No, dammit, don't go checking it out now. If there's anything I didn't get, it's because I couldn't find any, and you can tell me about it tomorrow and maybe we'll try somewhere else."

Billy nodded, nodded again to Judith. "See you," he said with a grin that revealed a really bad overbite, and, clutching the bag, disappeared out the door.

"Weird kid," Hovik said when he was gone. "I got to ask Joe Jack if all Pawnees are weird or is this one just a special case. I mean, I still can't decide if he's a genius or the last authentic nerd in California."

"Are you two still working on that loony project down at the creek?" Judith said. "Don't tell me you nearly got yourself shot getting wires and things for Billy to play with."

"You watch," Hovik said a trifle defensively. "We already got the creek dammed and the water wheel working, and Billy swears the generator's fixed now. Another week or two, we'll have electricity here. Then, by God, you'll see."

"I can see just fine now with the candles."

"The hell with that. I'm talking about that old Frigidaire in the kitchen building." He stretched out on the couch and smiled happily. "Gonna have me some cold beer this summer."

"Oh, God. You're doing all this just to chill that horrible home brew you and Billy—"

There was another interruption as the door banged open again and a small tornado, or perhaps an unusually noisy clump of tumbleweed, whirled and rolled into the room and across the floor. As it reached the center of the room it slowed and stopped, resolving itself into a couple of very small, very dirty, nearly naked children. The one on top seemed to be doing her best to split the other's head with a fist-sized rock. The one on the bottom had his teeth sunk in his opponent's leg. Indistinct curses and obscenities rent the air. Hovik watched fondly.

Judith said, "All right, all right, not in here. Susan, dump the rock and let your brother up. David, no biting."

They seemed inclined to continue. Hovik said in a normal voice, "Couple of rug monkeys about to get their little butts whacked."

The children separated reluctantly, glaring at each other. Susan said balefully, "He thwew my doll onto the woof."

"Did not. Ain't *theen* your Dod-damn doll."

"Hey, watch the language," Hovik said mildly.

"I *haven't* theen your Dod-damn doll."

"Better," Hovik nodded, closing his eyes.

"Out," Judith said firmly. "It's not dark yet. Go kill each other in the nice fresh air, all right?"

The children trotted toward the door. Susan, Hovik observed with one half-open eye, was still clutching her rock in a businesslike grip. As they disappeared their voices drifted back:

"Thtinky-panth."

"Wittle pwick."

"Twins," Judith said bleakly. "I wonder if Billy Blackhorse knows how to tie tubes."

Hovik made no response. She wondered if he had fallen asleep.

She stood looking at him for a moment, arms folded over her breasts. Ten years, and she still couldn't quite believe it. How did you two meet, Judith dear? Well, you see, it was the end of the world, and we—

She leaned against the wall, feeling the rough texture of the bearskin that hung there, and felt again the deep-running worry that had troubled her for weeks. Ten years, and it seemed to be getting too long for Hovik. He hadn't, she told herself, wandered into that ghost town alone through simple carelessness; Hovik didn't do things like that, whatever he said. It was just a new and more frightening manifestation of a restlessness that had been building in him for a long time, and she wondered what would come next. Well, she thought, you take a man who spent the first forty years of his life riding motorcycles, joining the Marines and getting kicked out, getting put in prison and breaking out, pulling holdups and stealing cars and God knows what else—you take a man like that and stick him with the responsibility of leading a tribe of refugees and survivors through the grimmest decade in human history, and after awhile give him a family to cope with besides, and what do you expect? A wonder the big bastard hadn't taken off long ago. . . .

Without opening his eyes Hovik said, "How long's it been now? Ten years?"

Judith jumped slightly. "Yes," she said. "You mean since—"

"Since it all went down." He sat up and gestured about him at the long room: the animal skins and blankets on the walls and floor, the candles in their holders, the weapons hanging everywhere. "I guess I mean since we been living like, you know, this."

He rubbed his eyes. "Yeah, I figured it had to be ten years. Four years here, then before that about six at that place we had down south, the old Resistance camp. Don't remember how long we spent in between, wandering around, after we got burned out down there."

He looked at her. "Jesus, Judith, you know I'm fifty years old? Where the hell did it *go*? I feel sometimes like—" He shook his head. "I don't know how the fuck I feel any more."

Good God, Judith thought with tired amazement, he's bored. He just had a fight to the death with four armed men, and he's bored.

Aloud she said, "Franklin Roosevelt Hovik. If you're starting to go middle-aged crazy on me—"

He laughed suddenly. "Okay, okay. Any chance of getting something to eat around here?"

As they walked toward the dining room together, he put his arm around her waist in a familiar bearlike movement. "Listen, talk about crazy," he said, "I'll tell you a weird one. Joe Jack talked to some drifters down on the highway yesterday, come up from down south. They claim somebody down that way, some bunch of paramils, got this train running. No shit," he said as she turned her head to stare at him, "a real train. Anybody'll believe that, they'll believe anything."

4

General James M. Decker (the M stood for Michener; his mother had read *Tales of the South Pacific* twice during her pregnancy and considered James Michener the greatest writer who had ever lived), formerly Major Decker of the Arizona National Guard and currently Commander in Chief of the Army of America, cleared his throat and said, "It would be presumptuous for me, or any other mortal man, to claim to have been personally chosen by the Almighty. Rather let me say simply that there came a time when I could no longer escape the conviction that I was to be an instrument of Destiny."

He paused and looked down at the bowed head of the young trooper who was scribbling rapidly at a yellow legal pad, trying to get it all down. "Capital D on Destiny, there, Private Hooten."

"Yes, sir," Private Hooten said somewhat desperately, scribbling. "Ah, do I capitalize the A in Almighty, too?"

"Of course," Decker said, and sighed. A fine-looking lad, but no secretary. What he wouldn't give for a genuine trained secretary who could take shorthand. Maybe he should have waited to begin dictating his memoirs until someone more competent could be found. On the other hand that might never happen, and at least this helped pass the time during these long stops while the track ahead was repaired.

"I had often had these feelings of a special mission in my life," he resumed, "well before the virus, or Plague as it has come to be called—capitalize Plague, Hooten—precipitated the final breakdown of civilization as we in America had come to know it. Paragraph."

The frantic scritch-scratch of the pencil indicated Hooten was having trouble keeping up. Decker turned and walked toward the metal stairway in the center of the compartment and mounted the steps to the observation deck of his private car. From here he could see down the length of the stopped train, either way; or, if he felt like wasting time on unproductive nonessentials, he also had a fine view of the mountains and the trees and such trifles.

He reached up and tapped the thick glass of the observation dome. Bullet-proof glass, supposedly, though he doubted it would stop anything heavier than small-arms fire. During the week-long battle for control of the Barstow yards, a few bullets had glanced off the thick glass while he fought the train from here, but he had no idea what caliber they might have been.

"Private Hooten," he called, "did you know that this car was originally built for the use of the last President of the United States?"

"I'd heard that, sir." Hooten's voice drifted up the stairs, still sounding harried. "I didn't know whether to believe it or not."

"Oh, yes, it's true enough, son." Decker chuckled. "Of course the late President never actually used it, never even saw it as far as I know—it was still in the yard, undelivered, when I found it and put it to use as my command center."

He smiled to himself. It had just occurred to him, though not for the first time, that the car was at last on its way to fulfilling something close to its original purpose. Maybe better, all things considered.

"Perhaps it would be well—can you hear me clearly, Hooten?"

"Yes, sir."

"Perhaps it would be well to observe at this point that this breakdown was in fact no more than the ultimate, some might even say the inevitable, development of a slower and more subtle breakdown that had been taking place in our country for a very long time. The last Administration had indeed done a great deal to try and arrest this deterioration, notably the much-needed expansion of Federal police powers, and a general get-tough policy against moral decay and treasonous dissent. Still, it was too little and too late."

He paused again to let Hooten catch up. Leaning on the chromed handrail, he surveyed the train, which always gave him pleasure. He had never given it a name, though the idea had crossed his mind now and again; there was no need. It was simply "the train" and there was no other, not at this time, not in this part of the world, perhaps not anywhere else on Earth. Oh, there were reports of pitiful efforts here and there about the country—wood-burning steam puffers, mostly, ancient tourist-bait contraptions revived and operated by lunatics with nothing better to do—but those were mere silly diversions. This wasn't transportation; this was a weapon.

Up at the head of the train, two big SD-9 diesels, former Southern Pacific units, supplied the motive power, their cabs and engines armored with welded-on steel plates taken mostly from old Wells Fargo and Brinks armored cars. He could have chosen bigger, newer locomotives, had had his choice from silent yards full of more powerful models, or he could have added another locomotive for more speed and added power on the steep grades; but more power meant more fuel consumption, and fuel was already a constant problem. And speed was not, after all, particularly important; the objective was still a long way off, but it had been there for over a decade and it wasn't going to go anywhere until they arrived.

Besides, they were already having to travel at a fraction of their potential speed, due to the poor condition of so much of the track. Right now, somewhere up ahead, the work crew was laboring to repair yet another damaged stretch; it was their second such halt today, and it was only a little after noon. Decker ground his teeth in momentary anger: stopping to deal with armed resistance was one thing, but this sort of petty tinkering was inglorious and frustrating. He hoped the fresh workers from the last little town would help speed the job.

He continued to look up and down the train. There had been various changes over the two years since he had put it together—new cars added and old ones dropped, a few lost through sabotage or accident or enemy action—but in spirit it was still the same train. Most of the cars had been modified for combat with the addition of improvised armor and mounted weapons, though the expendables—such as the old boxcars that carried the press-ganged civilian work crews—remained unaltered and unprotected. Piles of sandbags, lashed in place with steel cables, covered the tank cars carrying the precious diesel fuel; more sandbags surrounded the flatcar-mounted 105mm. howitzer and the quartet of heavy mortars. Near either end of the train, a heavy tank squatted aboard a drop-bed flatcar; it had been hell's own job getting those things in place, for their own engines had been beyond repair.

The whole thing, Decker thought with a surge of pride, might look like something out of the Russian Civil War or the Mexican Revolution, but it was surely the most powerful single military entity in California today, and tomorrow—

"Ready, sir," Hooten called.

Decker climbed back down the stairs, seeing Hooten's large brown eyes fixed expectantly on him, knowing he made an imposing figure even in the informal uniform—open-necked khaki shirt with four metal stars on each shoulder, khaki shorts, leather belt and holstered revolver—that he had chosen today. True, he was not tall; shorter than average, if anything, but he had always considered himself well-proportioned, and he kept in condition with the elaborate exercise equipment at the end of the compartment. If he had been vain enough to dye his hair, he thought, he could have passed for a man in his thirties. Actually he felt the sprinkling of gray hairs added to the image of authority.

Pacing back and forth before the metal desk where Hooten labored, Decker said, "Where was I? Too little and too late, yes. The heroic efforts of the President and others could not reverse the effects of generations of permissiveness and moral decadence. The decline in religious faith, family values, respect for authority, the manly virtues of—" He stopped, shook his head. "Strike that last sentence, Hooten. I think I want to go into those things in detail in the next chapter."

He looked at Hooten as the orderly scratched out a line. What a fine-looking soldier, he thought. Healthy outdoor complexion, strong jaw line, curly blond hair cut neatly to military style. Clean-shaven even though he couldn't possibly have anything much to shave yet. Make a fine model for a recruiting poster.

"Ah, let me see," Decker said. "New paragraph. Some have seen the Plague and the subsequent disasters as evidence of Divine intervention—yes, Hooten, capital D—or, as I have heard men say, the judgment of an angry God on a nation hopelessly lost in moral degeneracy. I myself am not qualified to say, being a simple fighting man rather than a theologian. However—"

He stopped and pressed his hand to his forehead for a moment. "All right, Hooten. I think we've done enough for now. Let's take a break, shall we?" He smiled at the orderly. "You must be tired. It's hot in here. Care for a glass of cold water?"

"Thank you, sir," Hooten said gratefully. "Where, uh—"

"In back, right down the passageway there. Sorry there's nothing to drink but water, but at least it's good and cold." Actually Decker had a well-supplied little bar in his quarters, but there was no way in hell he was going to waste rare whisky on an enlisted man. Probably too young to drink anyway. "Here, I'll show you."

He gestured for Hooten to precede him down the passageway. Watching the healthy movement of the orderly's solid-looking shoulders and narrow hips under the thin camouflage-patterned fabric, he thought what a fine physical specimen Hooten was, especially for an orderly on non-combat duty.

"You've kept yourself fit, I see, Hooten," he remarked. "I'll have to consider that when I make up the next promotion list, won't I? Here we are."

He opened the door of the little refrigerator and took out a pitcher. One of the little extra blessings of life aboard the train: the twin diesels' huge generators produced more than enough electricity to run a few civilized conveniences. True, his private car was the only one with working air-conditioning—and even it didn't work very well—but at least, on these warm days, he had ice for his drink. That alone, he sometimes felt, made it all worthwhile.

At Decker's direction Hooten got two glasses from the cabinet next to the refrigerator and poured. "Thank you, Hooten," Decker said. "Hooten, Hooten. Would that be a Dutch name? Hmm. What's your first name, Private Hooten?"

"Richard, sir."

"Richard, ah, yes. There was a very great King of England by that name, Richard, did you know that?"

"Uh, no, sir."

"No, suppose not." God, the boy would have been no more than a child when the books and the history classes went into the discard along with everything else. Not that American youth had ever shown much grasp of history. . . . Hooten probably didn't even know where England was, or what a king had been. "Richard the Lionhearted," Decker explained. "One of my lifelong heroes, along with Alexander the Great and Douglas MacArthur. Men of Destiny, all."

He smiled at Hooten, moving closer in the narrow passageway. "What do your friends call you, Richard? Dick? Rich?"

Hooten was smiling back, somewhat uncertainly. A very attractive smile, Decker thought. In a manly sense, of course. "Richie, sir," he said. "They call me Richie. Or sometimes just Rich."

"Richie, Richie. Well." Decker beamed at him. "Why

don't we step over here into my personal quarters, Richie . . . ?"

The Corporal in charge of Mackenzie's work crew said for possibly the twentieth time that afternoon, "Ahright, you sorry bastards, this ain't no God-damned picnic in the country, we ain't here to smell the flowers, move like you got a fucking purpose. Sooner we get this shit off the tracks, sooner we can all get back on the train, outta the hot sun."

Mackenzie listened expectantly, but for some reason this time the Corporal failed to add that he didn't want to see nothing but assholes and elbows. Maybe, Mackenzie thought with a glimmer of hope, the overgrown jackass was developing a sore throat.

He was right, though, about the hot sun; this had to be the warmest day of the summer so far. Mackenzie's eyes were stinging with sweat, but he knew better than to stop to wipe his face. So far the big Corporal with the big mouth had not personally inflicted any physical punishment, but some of the lower-ranking guards seemed to make a hobby of finding trivial pretexts to kick and curse the toiling prisoners. They never really injured anyone, Mackenzie noticed, not enough to impair the victim's ability to work, and they never kept it up long enough to disrupt the operation at hand, but it was still something to be avoided if possible. He blinked away the worst of the sweat and jabbed his long-handled shovel into the pile of rock and earth in front of him.

Actually the work wasn't all that hard in itself; he'd had to work this hard and harder, digging in the garden or chopping firewood, back at the mountain cabin. And this particular job was a relatively easy one: a minor earthslide, probably triggered by last year's quake or perhaps this spring's torrential rains, had dumped a half-ton or so of hillside across the tracks. There were no trees or big rocks in this one—unlike the horror on which they had broken their backs yesterday—and the rails underneath should still be all right; once the right of way was clear, they shouldn't have to do any track work.

The work wasn't so bad, but the pay scale left a lot to be desired. As did the hours, the accommodations, and the attitude of the management. . . .

There were eight of them in the work crew just now. There were many more prisoners back in the boxcars, but no doubt it had been considered that eight was the maximum number that could do a small-scale job like this without getting in each other's way. The crew was all male; Mackenzie had noticed that they rarely called out the women for track work or other heavy labor unless the job was so big they needed all available hands—as when they had had to repair that damaged trestle bridge the other day—and even then the men did the heaviest lifting. Mostly the women prisoners seemed to be employed in various tasks on the train itself: working in the kitchen car, washing clothes for the "soldiers," or general cleaning duties.

(And, Mackenzie assumed, there was also the traditional employment of captive women under such circumstances. So far he had not actually witnessed anything of the sort, but unless these camo-clad storm troopers were radically different from every other quasi-military bandit outfit in history, a certain degree of rape privilege would be considered one of the basic perks of enlistment. Men came from time to time and took women away, singly or in groups, and sometimes the women came back in a short time and sometimes they came back next morning, barely able to walk, and sometimes they didn't come back at all. He suspected that a good many of them sooner or later consented to anything that would get them out of the boxcars, and he couldn't blame them.)

Directly behind the work crew sat the point buggy. That was what the troopers all called it, anyway; actually it was just a flat-bed truck that had been modified to run on rails. Plates of rusty steel or iron had been welded about the cab and the engine—which, from the sound of it, seemed to be diesel—as crude armor; the bed was surrounded by a parapet of sandbags and steel rails. A fifty-caliber machine gun was mounted on a kind of pedestal, high enough to be able to fire forward over the cab. From the front jutted a weird-looking arrangement of iron pipe and lengths of rail that, with the big winch mounted on the front bumper, formed a crude but effective hoist for moving things too heavy for human muscle.

The point buggy, Mackenzie had learned, performed an extremely important function: running well ahead of the train, the men aboard watched the track ahead for obstacles or hazards or signs of hostile action, and signaled back to the train, he had not yet learned just how. It was a sound idea, he had to admit; the tracks were in really poor repair in some places, bad enough to cause a derailment, and he knew that a train like this, moving at any speed, could easily take half a mile to stop.

The crew of the point buggy also helped guard the labor details when there was track work to be done. Right now, Mackenzie was very conscious of that big fifty-caliber covering him and the others. Those half-inch slugs would literally blow a man to pieces at this range.

"Ahright, ahright," the Corporal was shouting, "what's the holdup here, shoulda been done already, I don't wanta see nothing but assholes and elbows—"

It was Mackenzie's fourth day on the train, if you counted the day he had been taken prisoner. It was hard for him to keep that in mind; it seemed sometimes that he had been on this train for a very long time. Time passed almost imperceptibly in the dark boxcar; to a degree he welcomed the labor details, despite the hard work and the abuse, simply because they got him out into the fresh air and the sunshine and gave him something to do to keep from going insane. Once he had been certified by NASA's experts as being able to handle confinement, sensory deprivation, and simple boredom better than most men, but that had been a long time ago and he had had reasons he believed in. . . .

Actually, the physical conditions in the boxcar were not as bad as they might have been; this was no cattle car to Auschwitz, no Siberian death train. The prisoners were, to all intents and purposes, slaves, but they were the labor force for a number of very important jobs—any attempt to make the troopers do much of this sort of work, Mackenzie suspected, would quickly result in numerous desertions and even mutiny—and, in this depopulated land, replacements would not be easy to obtain. It was only logical to keep the captives reasonably healthy.

The car, then, was not badly crowded; there was plenty of room to stretch out at night, and a plentiful supply of olive-drab blankets for the sometimes cool nights. There were two large steel barrels of fresh water at the forward end of the car, regularly refilled by a detail of prisoners; at the other end, a row of plastic buckets served as a crude latrine—

someone, probably the prisoners themselves, had rigged blankets as a screen, even though privacy was largely a forgotten concept here—and another detail kept them emptied.

There was even a fair amount of light and ventilation; the big sliding steel doors had been removed and replaced by a roughly welded but solid affair of iron bars, laced with lengths of barbed wire. Mackenzie guessed that this had been done to allow the guards to check on the prisoners without having to open the doors, rather than from any humanitarian considerations.

They were fed twice a day, morning and evening, lining up along the right of way beside the kitchen car, where women with big ladles dumped fairly adequate portions—corn-meal mush in the morning, a vile-looking and tasteless stew at day's end—into the various metal or plastic containers the prisoners held. The food vessels they had been issued on the first day of captivity—Mackenzie had gotten an empty coffee can; he was developing some promising thoughts about turning it into a weapon—were in fact the only possessions the prisoners had, and they tended to be irrationally protective of them; already he had seen one nasty confrontation, that had very nearly turned into a fight, over the ownership of an ordinary plastic salad bowl.

The train did not run at night; Mackenzie was surprised at first, but then he realized the condition of the tracks would have made night running dangerous, even assuming the lead locomotive's headlight still worked. Instead the train sat silent on the tracks—always, he observed, in a spot where it could easily cover the approaches with its heavy weapons—and a detachment of troopers disembarked and set up a defensive perimeter.

That was the quiet time, then, the long still nights when

Mackenzie could lie on his back on the boxcar floor that had finally stopped bouncing and jerking and swaying beneath him, and enjoy the silence, and try to think. Now and then a voice would call out in the darkness, the unintelligible cry of a man or woman having a bad dream; occasionally there would be sounds of someone moving about and then a trickling from back at the latrine buckets, and then more shuffling of feet and perhaps a muffled curse or two before things grew quiet again. Or there would be the crunch of boot-heels on gravel as one of the guards walked by outside; the valuable livestock in the boxcars was carefully watched, day and night. . . .

Mackenzie had so far made no acquaintances among the prisoners in his boxcar, had not even had any real conversation with any of his fellow slaves. Most of the people in this car seemed to be from the little town where he had been captured, and they were a clannish, suspicious lot; clearly they considered him as much an outsider as the train troopers. They were not exactly hostile; they simply ignored him altogether. The Invisible Man of Boxcar Three, Mackenzie thought now and then; perhaps he should wrap himself in bandages like Claude Rains.

But in fact he had no real desire to become involved with anyone here. He did not know yet how he was going to escape—dozens of ideas had come to mind, been considered and analyzed, as he waited out the nights, but so far nothing had looked all that promising—but when he did, it would be on his own, and he would take no one with him.

And he *would* escape; that was not even open to question. Long ago, as a young Marine pilot, he had been thoroughly trained in the principles and techniques of escape and evasion; he knew that the cardinal rule was never to accept captivity as anything but a highly temporary condition, to be terminated as quickly as possible. Once a prisoner fully accepted his situation, he was finished.

The escape-and-evasion instructor at Quantico, Mackenzie recalled, had often quoted a line from a book by a British officer who had masterminded a series of brilliant escapes during World War II. "I believe," the Englishman had written, "that there is no such thing as an escape-proof prison, save only that of the human identity. And at times I suspect even that is no more than a clever bit of propaganda on the part of the Warden."

"Ahright, *let's* go," the Corporal called monotonously. "*Put* your backs in it. What a buncha pussies."

In his private quarters, General Decker was saying, "Oldest of military traditions, Richie. Sacred comradeship of fighting men. Basis of all the great warrior societies. The Romans, the Janissaries, the Samurai, the Spartans. Oh, God, yes, the Spartans," Decker said, beginning to run out of breath. "Richard the Lionhearted. Achilles."

"Yes, sir," Richie said with some difficulty.

"Hold still, Richie."

"That wasn't me, sir. I think the train's starting to move again."

"Oh. Well, good, about time too. As you were, Richie," Decker said. "As you were. . . ."

5

The following morning, as the prisoners lined up in the gray half-light for the morning ration, a fat, bald, sweaty-faced man in a dirty white apron appeared in the doorway at the back end of the kitchen car. He looked upset about something.

"Need us a volunteer in here," he said in a high-pitched, almost childish voice. "You," he said, pointing a finger like a short pink sausage at Mackenzie, who was standing nearest to the kitchen-car steps. "You'll do. Get your ass in here."

Mackenzie climbed the dew-slick steps and followed the fat man into the long steam-filled kitchen, where a number of women and another fat man worked rapidly over stoves and sinks and metal counters. "Never mind that crap you were waiting on out there," he said to Mackenzie. "You do your job in here this morning, you'll get troops' rations. Over this way."

He showed Mackenzie a long sink full of large and dirty pots and pans. "You ever do any dishwashing?"

"A long time ago," Mackenzie said, remembering boot camp.

"Yeah, well, anybody can do this. There's the soap—it ain't much good, but it works if you scrub hard—and don't use any more hot water than you have to until we get rolling. This kitchen's all electric—the Old Man gets pissed off if we use too much juice while we're standing still. Once they get the big engines cranked up to traveling speed, it don't matter. Hell, you could run a fair-sized town on the electric power those things turn out."

Mackenzie nodded and reached for a brush. The fat man said, "I'm Bob. You got any problems or questions, check with me. Get to work and no grabassing around with the girls, they all got jobs to do too."

The soap was even weaker than Bob had said, and the water wasn't very hot, and the scrub brushes were worn out, but Mackenzie persevered and eventually began to see results. The train got under way with a lurch, slopping soapy water over him as he grabbed the sink for support. Bob laughed and did something at a control box and in a little while the water grew hotter.

It was hot in the narrow kitchen car and soon Mackenzie was soaked in sweat. He told himself it was still better than track work out in the sun, and Bob seemed to be considerably easier to work for than the guards. Then, too, there were all sorts of interesting possibilities; for one thing, it shouldn't be too hard to acquire some sort of weapon in here. The knives seemed to be kept locked in a stainless-steel drawer —he saw Bob taking the key from around his neck—but there were other utensils that wouldn't be hard to modify.

Bob came over, followed by a small dark woman in a white apron. She held a tray full of dishes and tableware.

"Stuff from the officers' table," Bob said to Mackenzie. "Rest of the troops have to look after their own eating equipment, thank God. Do one hell of a good job on this, because the Old Man's really got a thing about his personal stuff being clean. Get through with this, you can take a break and have some breakfast yourself."

Some time later Mackenzie sat at a table at the back of the car, eating. The troopers evidently did eat better than the prisoners, but only a little better. At least there was a bit more of it.

Bob the cook came and sat down opposite Mackenzie, holding a steaming cup. "This ain't real coffee, of course," he said conversationally. "The Old Man's got a little in his car, but nobody else has seen any in God knows when. This is just some imitation shit we made a while back, mostly roasted corn meal. Tastes awful, but you can have some if you want."

Mackenzie shook his head. Bob said, "Well, you ain't missing a damn thing, that's for sure. I'm just so used to having a hot cup of something in my hand, this time of morning, it don't matter what's in it." He grinned. "Did this all my life, you know? Cooked for the Santa Fe for years, then I had my own diner for a couple of years in Globe, Arizona, before it all went to hell."

He made a sad face. "Boy, there was awhile there, though, I didn't think I'd make it. That wasn't no time for a fat man, I'll tell you. I was about half starved by the time the General finally started putting the Army together. Didn't want me at first, till they found out I could run a kitchen and a railroad kitchen at that. I tell you one thing," he said, "people maybe say a lot of stuff about the Old Man, but they better not say it to my face."

Mackenzie made no reply. Bob rubbed his sweaty pink face and said, "Anyway, what I was gonna say, I like the way you work. This kid I had in here on the sink, he was looking a little green yesterday, now they tell me he didn't make it through last night—think he had a weak heart or something—so now I'm short-handed. You keep on working the way you been doing, I can fix it so you work here regular. It's long hours, but it beats fixing track, and you get three meals a day instead of two, and my crew don't have to pull any other details."

He jerked his thumb over his shoulder. "Kitchen crew's mostly all women, but I like to have one strong man around, because sometimes we got heavy stuff that needs lifting. In fact come on, you can help me move these bags of rice right now—"

Mackenzie worked all day in the kitchen car, washing pots and pans and "helping" the cook—which turned out to mean lifting and carrying everything bigger than a ten-pound bag of salt, while Bob watched and mopped his face and talked about the heat. The fat man seemed pleased with his efforts.

The new job, he decided, had real potential. Not only would it be simple enough to acquire a weapon, he could also steal food and other useful supplies for his escape. And the kitchen crew wasn't nearly as closely guarded as the outside workers; obviously Bob, like all good Mess Sergeants, ran his own little empire and was left largely alone.

If nothing better turned up, Mackenzie thought, he could simply leap out the kitchen-car door while the train was moving. He was pretty sure he could do it without serious injury, and by the time they got the train stopped—if they even went to that much trouble over one prisoner—he could be into the woods. A few shots might be fired at him from the train, but the odds were at least even that he could get away with it.

As he finished up the pots and pans from the noon meal, the small dark woman came up beside him and said, "Go sit down. I'll bring you your dinner."

He looked down at her, startled. He had not really looked at any of the women who had worked all around him; he had simply been too busy, or else he had been checking out escape possibilities. This one, he saw, was young, really just a girl: nineteen or twenty at most, and pretty in an undersized way. Black hair in braids, skin the color of a walnut rifle stock: Mexican or Indian, he thought, probably the latter. She had a distinct accent that didn't sound Hispanic.

She said, "Go on, it's okay. Bob don't care."

He nodded and walked down the center of the swaying car to the table at the rear. The train, he noticed, was moving at a good clip; they had not stopped at all so far today. So much for getting out of track work. But this was still better than sitting by the boxcar door for endless hours, waiting for something to happen.

She sat down across from him and rested her elbows on the table. "Go ahead, I already had dinner," she said as he dug his spoon into a bowl of beans and rice. "Not too great, sure, but at least we *get* dinner in here."

There were a few tiny bits of actual meat mixed in with the rice and beans, and some chopped-up wild onions to give it flavor. Mackenzie thought it was the best food he had had in days. The girl said, "Usually we eat a little better than this, when we're somewhere long enough to send out foraging parties, but lately seems like we're in this big hurry. Old Decker's sure got some kind of major wild hair up his ass."

"Decker?"

"You know, *General* Decker. Jesus Christ, man, you don't

know anything, do you? The crazy son of a bitch who runs this outfit."

She lowered her voice. "Somebody told me he wasn't a real General, but he sure as hell is now."

Mackenzie nodded. It was the first time he had heard the name; he had been wondering. The troopers all referred merely to "the Old Man" and the townspeople in his boxcar were as ignorant as himself.

The girl said, "My name's Alice Santana. What's yours?"

"Mackenzie." He could see no reason not to tell her; the name could not possibly mean anything to her. The last time he had been on a magazine cover, this girl would have been a small child, might not even have been born. "Ross Mackenzie," he said.

"Ross Mackenzie." She rolled her large dark eyes and whistled. "Fancy. Okay if I just call you Mac?" Mackenzie shrugged, his mouth full. "So where you from, Mac?"

Still chewing, he gestured in the direction of the window, at the sunlit countryside sliding past. They were out of the hill country now, passing through what had once been rich farmland and was now rolling grassy plains.

Alice Santana looked confused for a moment. "Oh—you mean you're from around here, California, huh? I'm from Arizona," she said. "Phoenix. Or was, till everything . . . you know. I'm Indian," she said in a different, suddenly guarded voice, looking closely at his face. "Full-blood Navajo."

He shrugged again. "So?" he said in a deliberately neutral voice, and saw her relax, the defensiveness leaving her eyes. He wouldn't have thought she'd be old enough to remember the prejudice and the discrimination, but maybe, he reflected, you didn't have to be very old to pick up on things like that. Not that there had been anything exactly subtle about the racism in the U.S. over the last decade before the breakdown; and Indians, toward the end, had been particularly hard hit.

"You got a set of prime shoulders on you, Mac," she said, looking him over with candid appreciation. "What were you in the old days, a wrestler?"

He said with a straight face, "I was an astronaut."

She burst into laughter. "All right, all right, I asked for that. Never ask anybody that kind of question, I know. Sorry." She shook her head, making her thick braids bounce. "Sense of humor, I like that. Most of these boxcar people, it's like they've already died inside their minds. Zombies, you know? Depresses me being around them."

Behind Mackenzie, Bob's voice said, "I hate to bust this up, Alice honey, but you got work to do."

"Sure, Bob." Alice got to her feet, not hurriedly, smoothing her threadbare white apron over equally threadbare jeans. "Hey, catch you later, Mac, okay?"

And she did catch him later: that evening, as the kitchen at last shut down and the guards came to take them back to the boxcars. As he stepped to the ground, hearing Bob locking up behind him, Alice appeared beside him and took his arm. "Long day," she said. "Come on, let's get off our feet."

He must have looked surprised. She said, "Hey, you don't want to go back to that damn cattle car you were in, do you? Kitchen crew always stays in this first one back here, on account of we're still cleaning up after the others get locked in." She tugged at his arm. "Anyway, don't you want to get better acquainted? Unless you got somebody waiting for you or something."

He walked with her and the rest of the kitchen staff, back along the stopped train. Alice said, "Boy, will you just look? What the hell *is* this place here, anyway?"

They were no longer out in the country, Mackenzie saw now; they were on the outskirts of a good-sized city. In the near distance he could see the gray blocky buildings of an industrial district and, beyond, the spread-out skyline of the city itself. He studied the view for a moment. "Sacramento," he said finally, amazed. "That's got to be Sacramento."

A guard, passing close to them, looked up. "That's right," he said, giving Alice a familiar grin. "This here's Sacramento, all right. Gonna stop here outside of town for the night, then get into the yards in the morning. The Old Man don't like to stop in the middle of a yard or a big town—too much cover for anybody that wants to jump us in the night."

"Sacramento," Alice said as the guard moved on. "How about that. Then what was that other good-sized town we passed through this afternoon?"

"Stockton," Mackenzie said absently. "If this is Sacramento, then that was Stockton. I'll be damned."

He was thinking that this was faintly ridiculous: the great and terrible armored train, for God's sake, was just now getting into Sacramento. He could have traveled almost as fast on his bicycle. Of course, they had lost a great deal of time clearing the track, repairing that bridge, and so on; still, the train didn't seem to be setting any speed records.

They had come to an open boxcar door. The other prison cars, he saw, were already sealed for the night, just as she had said. Another possibly useful bit of information. . . . In fact, he had already observed that security was considerably looser for the kitchen workers. Even the guards who herded them back along the train and into the car seemed to regard their assignment mostly as an opportunity to fraternize with the women, and cop a quick feel or two helping them into the car.

"Here we are," Alice said. "Give me a hand, will you, Mac?"

"I been on the train over a year now," Alice said, settling herself against him in the darkness. "Sometimes it feels like I been riding this damn train my whole life."

It was night, now, a dark overcast night, only a little dim light coming through the barred and barbed-wire doorway. Mackenzie sat with his back against the steel side of the boxcar; Alice sat beside him, her head resting against his chest. His arm was around her shoulders. She had seemed to expect that.

He had wondered at first just what she did expect. Since burying his wife, he had had no thoughts of sex whatever; that whole area had been blank, like so many other switched-off parts of his life. . . . But the Navajo girl had seemed to want nothing more than to be held, and to talk.

She had grown up in Phoenix, she said, where her family had had to move after the government shut down the last reservations. She had been nine years old when the Plague broke out—Mackenzie grinned to himself in the darkness: his guess had been right—and she did not remember much of how she and the surviving members of her family had escaped from the city. Eventually they had joined a group of Indians, Mexicans, and mixed-bloods in the mountains near Flagstaff. Some years later she had "married" an Apache boy who subsequently died after a fall from a horse.

Finally, a few years ago, she had headed back toward Phoenix with her older brother—hoping, she said, to find other surviving relatives—and been taken in, or rather captured, by a strange community on the edge of the desert.

"They called it a 'commune,' " she said, "but it was more like a, what do you call it, a concentration camp. Barbed wire, dogs, armed guards, you wouldn't believe that place. This bunch of total nut cases ran everything, and they had these goons they called the 'New Age Guard' walking around keeping everybody in line. I mean, they carried these big-ass clubs, knock the shit out of you as soon as look at you. Had their heads shaved, wore these boots and all. And after they whacked you, you were supposed to say, 'Thank you, Guardsperson, for the correction.' You didn't, they'd hit you some more."

The leaders of the commune, as best Mackenzie could gather, had operated according to a demented mixture of radical communism, pseudo-Eastern mysticism, and a certain level of outright lunacy. "Work your ass off all day in these God-damned fields," Alice said, "the stuff they grew didn't amount to shit because they had some crazy ideas about farming too—believe it or not, they'd line a bunch of people up in the field and make them sing these weird songs to the plants, supposed to make them grow better—then at night they'd make you listen to these long lectures or sermons till around midnight. Sometimes they'd read from this book by some asshole named Chairman Mao, sometimes it was stuff about Buddhism, sometimes they'd just be one of the head crackpots up there ranting on and on, whatever came into his head. You better stay awake and look interested, too, because the guards loved to belt you across the kidneys if you started to nod.

"No meat," Alice said, "no eggs or anything, just this godawful slop that was supposed to be good for you—even if it was, they barely gave you enough to stay alive on—no smoking, no booze, Christ, you weren't even allowed to *sing* except in the organized group singing. No sex, either, except when the leaders picked out a couple and told them to go make a baby—men and women stayed in separate quarters, women had to stay all covered up when men were around, couldn't even wear shorts in that heat, *shit*. Of course," she said bitterly, "there were some of the leaders went by different rules—hell, a couple of them seemed to be trying to fuck their way through the whole commune—but that was okay because they were helping you be a better person or something."

She shifted her body slightly. They had spread a blanket under them for a certain amount of protection—that's all I need now, Mackenzie had thought, a splinter in my ass from this chewed-up old wooden floor—but the floor was still very hard.

"And of course the guards, they got to do it to anybody they wanted, any time. They got to do *anything*—the leaders just didn't want to know. If you pissed them off enough they'd put you in this tiny little box of a thing, sheet metal, too small to stand up or stretch out in, and let you cook in the hot sun and freeze at night for a few days—'meditation therapy' was what they called it—or, if they happened to feel like it, they'd just kill you. Beat you to death with those damn clubs. I saw them do it, more than once."

"God," Mackenzie said. "It sounds like Cambodia."

"What's that?"

"Never mind. Go on. What finally happened?"

She turned her head and looked up at him. "Why, General Decker happened, that's what happened. By then he was happening to a whole lot of people, all over Arizona and

New Mexico. Those bastards with their New Age Guards," she said, "they thought they were hot shit, talked all the time about their big-deal revolution that was going to take over the whole world, but man, Decker's boys hit them like a herd of wild horses going through a cornfield. Took about half a day before it was all over. Well, and then another day for the hangings. I'll tell you something," she said, "I've seen a lot of people killed in my lifetime, but that was the only time I ever really enjoyed it."

"Decker hanged the leaders of the commune?"

"And all the guards that were still alive. Made a little speech about how normally there'd be a firing squad, but Communists didn't deserve an honorable death. Good old Decker," she said, "he'd finally found some real Communists. Probably made his whole week."

"But then," Mackenzie said after a moment, "he took the rest of you as his own prisoners, didn't he? I suppose it was still a change for the better, but—"

"Oh, yeah, sure, some liberator. But you got to remember, most of us were pretty damn helpless by that time—they'd jerked us around so we couldn't so much as take a shit without permission. We wouldn't have lasted a week on our own, and a lot of the poor bastards, you know, they'd been brainwashed so bad they still believed in that New Age Revolution crap. So I guess Decker did have some justification at the time, not that he ever seems to worry about stuff like that."

Mackenzie said, "He had the train then?"

"He had it, sort of. Just one engine, a few cars, no big guns yet, and he didn't have all that many men. He was already calling it the Army of America, though. Son of a bitch always has thought big."

Mackenzie nodded to himself. He had already calculated,

from what he had seen so far, that the Army of America might just possibly add up to an understrength battalion, no more. Of course, by post-Plague standards, that was an enormous force, especially with the added firepower of the train's heavy weapons.

"And you've been with them ever since," he said to Alice. "Never tried to escape?"

"Escape? Escape to what?" She laughed shortly. "Hell, I could have taken off a long time ago—they all know me, half the guards on this train tried to get into my pants at one time or another, and don't ask if any of them made it. I've been out after lockdown plenty of nights, by myself, no big deal. But what the hell? Take off alone, one little half-size girl, out in the middle of the desert or the mountains? Or like now, in some creepy old town full of God knows who and what? No, thanks."

She twisted within the curve of his arm to look him in the face. "You maybe got the wrong idea about how it works," she said. "Sure, we're all prisoners—I guess you could even call us slaves—but a lot of us, the ones that been with the train a long time, it's sort of something we're part of, you know? Bad as it is, it's what we've got, and at least it means steady meals and a place to sleep and a hell of a strong outfit to protect you. Oh, it's different if you're on the road gangs—Christ, they just use those poor bastards up and throw them away—but for the regular workers, like the kitchen crew, well, it could be worse."

She poked his chest with a stiff small finger. "And you better understand this: there are things out there, a *lot* of things, so much worse than this train you wouldn't believe it. Where you been for the last few years, off in the mountains or something?"

"Off in the mountains," Mackenzie said. "Yes, you could say that."

"Well, don't go passing judgment on people till you know what's happening, then," she said darkly. "I mean, that place where I was, that's not the only crazies-from-hell scene around. This girl who waits on the officers' table, we picked her up down by Bakersfield—she'd been with this bunch of religious weirdos who ran around in sheets and made human fucking *sacrifices*, if you're ready for that, to this god or spirit or something called Harry Krishna."

Mackenzie could think of nothing to say. She turned back and snuggled again into her original position.

"It was just last winter," she said, "that Decker all of a sudden got this big hard-on about California. I mean, we'd been running all over Arizona and New Mexico and up into Utah once—these Mormons pretty much handed us a bloody nose up there, though—kicking ass and picking up recruits and so on, but we were down in Tucson, everybody assumed it was just to spend the winter somewhere warm, and all of a sudden things got wild. They were doing all this work on the train, fixing it up for some heavy shit, man, had these prisoners filling sandbags and we had to stock up on food and all, nobody knew what the hell was happening but by then Decker could have got most of these guys to follow him to take on an earthquake or wrestle a tornado, you know? And then a few months ago he fell everybody in and made this long speech, nobody understood more than about a quarter of it but it was all about Destiny and how we were going to change history and save America and so on, and after that we all got on the train and headed west and, well, you know."

Mackenzie didn't know, not nearly as much as he would

have liked to know, but she seemed to be getting tired of talking.

She said suddenly, "You want to do it?"

"Do it?"

"Jesus, Mac, you know. *Do* it," she said impatiently. "Get laid. Fuck."

"Oh," he said, stupidly. "Ah. Hm."

She dropped one hand to his lap and groped briefly. "Nope, you must not have been thinking very hard about it. Either that or you got a real problem, been out in the mountains too long."

He said, "Look, Alice, don't get me wrong, but this isn't exactly a private bedroom here."

Alice snorted. "Doesn't seem to bother anybody else."

She had a point. Now that Mackenzie noticed, the dark interior of the boxcar was fairly alive with various rustlings and gruntings and groanings, so much heavy breathing it almost seemed he could feel a breeze. The effect was embarrassing rather than stimulating, at least to Mackenzie. He said, "Good God."

"Actually," Alice said, "it's not as bad as it sounds—noises kind of get noisier inside this tin can—but still, don't let the shortage of privacy stop you if you get to feeling friendly."

She settled her head into the hollow of his shoulder, laughing softly. "Hey, relax, Mac, I'm just having fun with you, I'm not gonna rape you." She took his arm and pulled it closer about her. "All I really want tonight is just to be held, like this. I'm not horny, Mac, I'm just a long way from home and feeling a little scared."

But later that night, some time between midnight and dawn, Mackenzie was suddenly jerked from sleep by a deafening blast of gunfire just outside the boxcar. He sat up with a lurch, fighting to orient himself, the girl beside him momentarily forgotten.

The noise was coming from all directions, he realized now: the banging and popping of rifles, the knock knock knock of machine guns and the deeper slam of the heavy fifty-calibers, and here and there sharp explosions that he thought must be grenades. Somewhere, he thought in the next boxcar, someone was screaming in pain or fear or both, a scream so high it almost touched the limits of the audible. Something hit the side of the boxcar with a clang.

Alice was saying, "Jesus Christ, Jesus Christ," and then something in a language Mackenzie didn't recognize. She sounded on the verge of hysteria.

From the doorway a man's voice said, "Everybody in there, stay down, lay flat on the floor. We're getting hit."

Someone inside the boxcar called out a question. The man outside said, "Don't know yet who it is, probably just some local creeps. Don't think it's anything heavy, but you people stay down anyway."

From up near the engines there was the coughing twin thump of a pair of heavy mortars. A moment later a great white light burst the night into harsh blacks and whites. Mackenzie saw men running, firing weapons.

Good thinking, he thought objectively, firing illumination rounds. The chorus of gunfire rose quickly, spiked with a few excited shouts. The mortars were firing more star shell, driving back the darkness. There was a sudden enormous boom as a howitzer went off and the train shook briefly with the recoil. An ear-splitting crack and the shriek of a high-velocity shell indicated at least one of the tanks was getting in on the action.

Whoever the attackers were, Mackenzie thought, they had to be insane, or terminally stupid, or at best catastrophically ignorant of what they were doing and what they were up against. From the sounds of the fire fight, it was clear that they had no weapons larger than rifles, and the sporadic and widely dispersed fire did not suggest a disciplined, well-planned attack.

Alice was trembling violently against him, and he put his arms around her. It was an almost automatic gesture, meant to be no more than a calming one, but she reacted instantly and with astonishing strength, clutching at him with wiry small fingers, pressing her body to his as if trying to get inside his skin. She was making a tiny animal sound in her throat, her breath hot on his neck.

He became aware of the points of her firm little breasts growing hard against his chest, while her pelvis began a slow hunching grind and her breath quickened. Almost immediately he was also aware of his own stiffening response, a rampant, mindless erection that threatened to burst through his pants and attack on its own.

They clawed and fumbled in the darkness, at each other's clothing, at their own, breaking buttons and fingernails, rolling over and over on the blanket, no longer feeling the hard rough floor. She raised her bottom with an impatient bucking motion as he tugged the ragged jeans down and, kicking to free her ankles and grasping him tightly in one hand, pulled him down and clasped him to her.

It was a crazed, brutal business, having nothing to do with love and very little to do with the usual forms of lust. They heaved and clutched and humped and breathed noisily through their mouths with audible grunts; both of them were bleeding from tiny scratches from nails and teeth and the floor. Later,

Mackenzie reflected that if the act had resembled anything in nature, it could only have been the mating of two wolverines. At the moment of climax she cried out something in that brittle-sounding language that he took to be Navajo. There was no attempt at silence or concealment, even though the light from star shells and tracers came in the doorway and illuminated their working bodies in black-and-white relief; all through the interior of the boxcar, similar scenes were being played in various combinations. . . .

And outside the fire fight continued to boom and bang and rattle and flash across the dark fields and along the weed-grown right of way, as the Army of America defended its train.

6

Hovik said, "What we need is some dynamite. You ask me."

Billy Blackhorse said, "Dynamite?"

"Yep." Hovik wiped sweat from his forehead and adjusted his headband. "God *damn*, I'm getting this hair cut short for the summer and if Judith don't like it . . . uh huh, dynamite. Or some plastic or even some God-damned ammonium nitrate. Some serious explosives, anyway."

From behind them Joe Jack Mad Bull said, "What's this about dynamite?"

They turned to look up at Joe Jack, who was clambering down the steep rocky bank of the creek, looking interested. He said, "You back to blowing things up, Hovik? Sounds like old times."

Hovik winced. "Don't remind me of that shit," he growled. "No, just look at this."

He stood atop a heap of loose rock and dirt and pieces of root, leaning on a pick. Beside him, Billy Blackhorse jabbed dispiritedly at the creek bank with a shovel. Joe Jack said, "My Native American ass, you two still jacking around with this mess? Looks like the awkward squad of the Corps of Engineers here."

Hovik sighed. "I know, I know. It seemed like such a simple idea, though." He threw down his pick and looked disgusted. "I thought we had it whipped, too, but it just wasn't strong enough."

"The generator and the rest of it," Billy Blackhorse added, "that's all fixed up now, ready to go, if we could just get this thing dammed up solidly so we could get a good head of water pressure on the wheel." To Hovik he added, "Look, it's going to be all right, it's just going slow—"

"Too damn slow," Hovik grunted. "Time we move that much earth with hand tools, it'll be winter and the creek'll freeze. Anyway, there's too much else needs doing around here. I can't justify spending that much time and labor on something we don't really have to have. Judith's already on my ass about fixing the roof."

"So," Joe Jack said, trying not to laugh, "what do you want with dynamite? Blow the whole thing to hell just out of disgust?"

"Well, I might be tempted . . . no, I was just wishing, like it seems I've spent the last ten years wishing for stuff you can't get any more. Just a few sticks of Du Pont, we could get this job finished in no time."

Billy Blackhorse was looking thoughtful. "Dynamite," he said in a faraway voice. "Let's see, I could—"

"No you couldn't," Hovik and Joe Jack said almost in unison.

"But listen—"

"You listen," Hovik said grimly. "You're a nice kid, Billy, and I like you. So don't even start *thinking* about trying to make dynamite, or TNT, or black fucking powder, or anything like that, because if I find out about it before you blow yourself to shit, I'm not going to enjoy what I'll do to your ass, and you won't enjoy it either."

Billy nodded reluctantly, a hurt look on his acne-scarred brown face. Joe Jack said, "He's right, Billy. It's not worth it."

"Let's knock off," Hovik said. "We're not doing shit here. Maybe we'll think of some other answer later, I don't know, a windmill or something."

Walking back up the road together, watching Billy Blackhorse disappear into one of the cabins ahead, Hovik said, "What a weird kid."

"Kid?" Joe Jack said. "Hell, Hovik, he's, what, twenty-five or so at least."

"Yeah, I know, but you can't help thinking of him—" He grinned at Joe Jack. "He reminds me of this boy who lived on my block when I was about twelve, his daddy owned the drugstore, got this chemistry set for Christmas. His folks spent the next year or so shitting bricks, he kept causing fires and smoking out the family and damn near blowing up the block."

"What finally happened to him?" Joe Jack said, laughing.

"Last I heard," Hovik said, "he was grown by then, he had this real good-paying job with the Teamsters' Union."

"Hm. Listen," Joe Jack said, "believe it or not, I picked up another story about that mysterious train. . . ."

The morning after the fight outside Sacramento, Mackenzie stood by the boxcar door, waiting for the guards and looking out at the area beyond the tracks. There were no particular signs of the previous night's violence, that he could see; no bodies lay in the grass and there were no shell holes. Down by the right of way he could make out a brassy gleam that must be ejected cartridge cases; that was all. The troops seemed to be going about their business as usual, perhaps a little more clumsily after a sleepless night, perhaps holding their weapons a little more at the ready, and there was a sharp smoky smell in the air.

Beside him, fiddling with her clothing, Alice said, "Go on, say it."

"What?"

"Whatever it is you're going to say. About last night." She stared up at him, her face unreadable, as he turned to look at her. "What we did. You're gonna say *something* sooner or later, so get on with it."

"Oh." He hesitated and then laughed. "Actually, the only thing that comes to mind is something I read about Mussolini—"

"Who the hell was he? Was he an Indian?"

"No, no. A low-grade dictator," Mackenzie said, "ran things in Italy a long time ago, made such a mess of it his own people finally shot him. What I read," he went on, grinning at her, "you see, the guerrillas who were going to shoot him, they had him in this hotel room while they decided what to do with him. They also had this woman who was his mistress—Clara, I think was her name, Clara Petacci—locked up with him. Well, when they came to get them, suddenly she said, 'Wait a minute,' and started to go back into the room, and when they asked what she was going back for, she said, 'My panties.' "

"You're making this up," Alice said suspiciously.

"No, no, I swear, this was in a history book, this happened. And of course, you know, the question is, what were they doing in there in those last minutes that she had them off?"

Mackenzie shook his head, laughing. "The only possible answer is that the old bastard just figured if he was about to go out, might as well get in one more quickie. Always thought it was the only classy thing he ever did."

"Jesus." Alice blinked rapidly. "I'll never understand white people. So what's your point?"

"Just," Mackenzie said more quietly, "I think it's probably a basic human instinct. Maybe it's something nature does to try to keep the species going, maybe it's just a way of releasing tension and fear, I don't know. All I mean is that it doesn't necessarily have anything to do with anything else. It's just something that happens. Last night it happened to us."

"Huh." She grabbed him around the waist and hugged. "Look, Mac, speak for yourself. For me, I'll by God tell you whether something's got anything to do with anything or not. Also," she said, seeing the guard coming, "your fly's open."

They spent all that day and part of the next in Sacramento, working their way into the big railroad yards—Mackenzie's mind boggled at the sight: acres of silent, rusting cars, still lined up on the rusty weed-grown tracks as if waiting for an engine and a crew to begin making up a train—and sitting parked for hours while one of the SD-9's shunted cars back and forth in an intricate series of chesslike moves and sweating troopers threw switches in response to shouted orders. Whatever Decker's problems, Mackenzie thought, he had somewhere acquired a genuinely brilliant engineer and train crew.

There was more waiting, when the way was finally opened,

while the train took on fuel from the yard's enormous storage tanks. Gasoline might be scarce as gold and considerably more valuable, yet apparently there was still a fair supply of diesel fuel remaining. It puzzled Mackenzie, but then he considered that there would be relatively few people with a need for the stuff—diesel automobiles had never been popular in the United States, and the big diesel trucks would not have many uses in the present world—those who did use them could have supplied their modest needs for years without heavily depleting the contents of the huge railroad-yard tanks. Even, he thought, if they succeeded in getting at the fuel; as it was, with the yard's pumping facilities useless, Decker's people had to do something complicated with a jury-rigged system of their own, and even then it was obvious that the flow was very slow.

And yet the fuel tanks still represented a form of great wealth to anyone who controlled the area—if nothing else, there were surely farm communities that would trade any quantity of food for a few barrels of tractor fuel—so perhaps that was one reason for last night's attack. . . . He suggested as much to Bob, who nodded. "We have to fight a lot for these places," the fat man said. "You shoulda seen the battle we had down at Barstow."

While the fuel trickled into bunkers and tank cars, other men swarmed over the yard, came back with unidentifiable hardware, made various repairs, and did other things to the train. It was all done with great efficiency; it was clear they had done all this many times before.

They spent the night in the yards, a nervous, uneasy night with all defenses ready and everyone expecting gunfire at any moment, but the attackers did not return. Around midnight there was a false alarm, probably a trooper firing at shadows, and the mortars fired a couple of star shells and everyone in the boxcars lay flat and cursed and prayed, but that was all.

Alice slept close beside him, curled up with one arm across his chest, but by now they were both too tired to do anything but sleep. Waking once during the night, feeling her next to him, he found himself speaking his wife's name; and then he remembered, but he fell asleep again before he could think it over.

The following day, a little before noon, Mackenzie finally got his first good look at General James M. Decker.

They were still sitting in the Sacramento yards, though it was obvious they would soon be moving out; the clumsy fueling setup had been dismantled and stowed in the maintenance car, and the troopers had been running about in the usual helter-skelter of such times, pulling in from the perimeter positions, while up ahead the lead engine, done playing yard goat, was once again coupled to its mate. It was the slack time of morning for the sink man, the breakfast pots cleaned and stowed and not much to do until after dinner; not much even then, today, for the troopers had been issued cold rations, some sort of dry tasteless survival bars, while the train was in the yards.

But then suddenly Bob came hurrying toward the sink and shoved a stack of pots and pans at Mackenzie. "Wash these," he said urgently, "and I *know* they're already clean, but wash 'em anyway. The General's on his way, and it don't do for him to see anybody standing around idle. Make a bunch of suds and scrub like a son of a bitch while he's here, he'll be happy and then we'll *all* get to be happy."

Amused and irritated, Mackenzie ran water and made suds, thinking: for God's sake, even after the end of the world, it never stops. . . .

A few minutes later the door at the end of the car snapped open. A husky, blond-haired, baby-faced young man in camouflage uniform stepped into the kitchen car, shouting something completely unintelligible. He was followed, then, by a khaki-clad individual who had to be the General.

Watching out of the corner of his eye, Mackenzie saw a rather small man, about his own age he thought, very neat-looking and stiffly erect in posture. No doubt he believed himself to look very martial, and perhaps it worked on the troops; to Mackenzie, however, the overall effect was that of a high-school vice-principal stalking the hallways looking for kids without passes. Or maybe the personnel manager of a minimum-wage sweatshop in a border town. . . . The visored cap with the gold braid, and the pistol in the gleaming leather holster, did help somewhat.

And for God's sake, he was carrying a swagger stick. Mackenzie was just as glad his back was turned so the General couldn't see his face.

Evidently Decker was merely checking with Bob about the food supply, rather than making an inspection; he stood in close conversation with the fat man for some time, while the baby-faced trooper made notes on a small pad. At the end, however, he walked quickly up and down the center of the car, looking around him in a casual way, making small sounds of satisfaction. He seemed to pause for a moment to look at Mackenzie, but then he moved on. Standing in the middle of the car, he said in a loud voice, "Well, Bob, you're doing a fine job as always. Let me know if you need anything.

Valuable man to us all, Bob, don't think you're not appreciated," he smiled, gesturing with his swagger stick. "You know the old saying, an army travels on its stomach."

Under his breath Mackenzie said, "Funny, you don't look Corsican."

He had not meant to speak aloud; he cursed himself mentally for doing so.

There was a bad pause while Decker's neck turned red and the swagger stick whacked sharply three times into his left palm. But then Decker suddenly smiled again, not very widely, and his shoulders shook briefly in what was evidently a silent laugh.

"Carry on," he said to Bob, and headed for the door, trailed by the baby-faced orderly. The door slammed shut behind them and everyone in the kitchen exhaled.

"You're crazy," Alice said to Mackenzie a moment later as she passed. "For a white man, you could almost have made it as an Indian."

The train pulled out of the Sacramento yards just after midday, moving slowly at first, halting for a number of switches that had to be thrown and, once, while the point-buggy crew shoved a burned-out city bus off the tracks. As it cleared the city Mackenzie studied the view out the windows and the angle of the shadows and concluded they were still moving north. That surprised him; he had assumed they were going to San Francisco or the Bay area—the old Oakland Army Terminal, if anything was left of it, ought to be a logical target for a man like Decker—or over the mountains to Reno, or even back the way they had come. He could think of nothing in the rugged, thinly settled interior of northern California to interest this strange gang of rail-borne paramils. Even if they were merely cruising aimlessly around the country looking for action—which he didn't believe for an instant; there was clearly some definite goal in Decker's mind, however exotic his style—they wouldn't find much of it this way.

On the other hand, it was excellent country in which to escape. Mackenzie began to watch and calculate again. Perhaps when they got into the mountains . . .

But as the train rolled through the countryside beyond Marysville, the young orderly with the childish face came into the kitchen and spoke to Bob, and the fat cook nodded and came over and tapped Mackenzie on the shoulder.

"Go with Corporal Hooten here," he said. "The Old Man wants to see you in his private car."

When Mackenzie came in, Decker was sitting behind his desk looking at a 9mm. automatic pistol, wondering how hard it would be to make up a pair of handles inset with the stars of a General. He had seen a picture of George Patton wearing a pistol like that, and it struck him as a neat-looking idea. Perhaps one of the troopers might have the necessary skills.

Mackenzie said, "You sent for me." It was no more than a statement.

"Ah, yes." Decker put the pistol on his desk and looked at the man in front of him. Average-sized man, impressive upper-body development, graying hair, shabby clothing, damp from sweat and kitchen steam: all in all not a very striking sight, though there was something in the eyes that made Decker look a second time. He was standing straight and his arms were at his sides, but he was definitely *not* standing at attention—even though Decker felt certain that this man could stand at attention like a West Point drill instructor if he chose to do so.

He said, "Your name?"

"Mackenzie." No "sir," either. Never mind, that could be dealt with later. "Ross Mackenzie."

"Mackenzie. Scottish name, of course. Great warrior race, the Scots. Have you any military experience, Mackenzie?"

A hesitation. "Yes."

"Branch of service?"

"Marine Corps."

"Ah!" This was promising; like most Army officers, Decker had a secret but profound admiration for the Marines. "An officer, perhaps?"

"Yes." Good God, the man was giving away absolutely nothing. Decker said a little impatiently, "Have you ever led troops in combat, Mackenzie?"

Again that hesitation. "Not in the sense you mean," Mackenzie said finally. "In fact I've never led troops, in your sense, at all. Aviation," he explained. "I was a Marine pilot."

"Oh." Decker had thought for a minute the man had been a *real* officer. "Too bad, Mackenzie, I'd give anything for experienced, properly trained infantry officers right now. Even so," he said, "you must have had some degree of training in this sort of thing. I understand the Marine Corps requires all its people, even pilots and technical personnel, to train first as rifle-carrying Marines."

"True. But my only combat experience was in the air, in the Middle East."

"Ah, teaching manners to our raghead brothers, eh? Good man, good man." Decker leaned back in his chair and put his hands on the desk top. "Well, in any case, you're obviously in fine physical condition, especially for a man your age—how old *are* you, Mackenzie?"

"Forty-seven."

"Really? I'd have put you at a few years younger than myself—I'm forty-five, you know," Decker added, knocking off half a dozen years on general principles. "Anyway, as I was saying, you're undoubtedly a man of superior intelligence, just to have qualified as a jet pilot, and you've at least had basic military training in an elite fighting organization. It's absurd that you've been wasted all this time as a menial laborer, of course, but we can set that to rights immediately."

He tapped his fingers on the desk and made a rueful face. "Normally I make a point of speaking with each new group of civilian workers, explaining our mission and offering any able-bodied men the opportunity to enlist in the Army of America—why, I'd imagine half the troops on this train right now joined us by that route—but we're on a rather special operation now, Mackenzie, having to travel long distances in new and sometimes hostile territory, and I simply haven't had time. Anyway, with all that damage to the tracks down south, we needed every available worker."

He stopped. After a moment Mackenzie said, "Am I to take this as a job offer? You want me to be one of your, ah, soldiers?"

"Come now, Mackenzie." Decker stopped smiling. "Don't be deliberately obtuse. I'm offering you much more than a uniform and a rifle—right now I've got plenty of troops for what we have to do. What I'm offering," he said impressively, "is a commission in the Army of America."

"You want me to be an *officer* in this outfit?" Decker saw

a twitch at the corner of Mackenzie's mouth, as if the man was trying not to laugh. "I'm a little old for a platoon leader, don't you think?"

"Ah, hell, Mackenzie." Decker snorted in irritation. "Don't you see my problem here? I need an executive officer, somebody to help me run this outfit, keep things moving, attend to all these little details so I can concentrate on the Big Picture. People who can kill people are a dime a dozen nowadays—that's about the only kind of people who survived the years after the Plague. I've been looking for a man who can think."

"I see." There was definitely something insubordinate going on at the corners of Mackenzie's mouth. "May I ask, General—is this an enlistment offer or am I being drafted?"

Decker frowned. "Does that mean what it sounds like?"

"Probably." Mackenzie shrugged, looking straight at Decker. Didn't the Marines teach their pilots *anything* about military courtesy? "If the option's open, I'd rather pass."

Decker put his elbows on the desk and folded his hands together and leaned forward, resting his chin on his knuckles. "You don't want to serve your country in these terrible times, Mackenzie? What sort of American are you?"

This time it was Mackenzie's turn to snort, openly and scornfully. "For God's sake, General, what the hell country are you talking about? I haven't seen any signs it's still around. Maybe as a memory, as an ideal—"

"You listen, Mister." Decker's voice was suddenly low and penetrating; he fought to get control of a slight tremor. "The United States of America has never died. The United States of America *will* never die. Never question that. Almost as well say that God is dead."

Mackenzie shrugged again, looking unimpressed. "The

United States, in any sense that was ever worth anything, died years ago, long before the Plague," he said flatly. "It died when the greedheads and the manipulators and the power junkies got control of it and the people let them get away with it. Come to think of it," he added drily, "you could probably make out a case that the same people also knocked off God."

He stared down at Decker with his cold pale eyes. "Oh, and let's not forget the tinhorn soldiers," he said. "Present company excepted, let's hope."

Decker's hand was trembling as he picked up the pistol from his desk. "You realize I've had men shot for saying less than you've just said?"

Mackenzie's eyes shifted to a point somewhere over Decker's head. "So go ahead and shoot me," he said in a bored voice.

There was a stomach-burning second in which Decker almost did it; his thumb began to push the pistol's safety lever to firing position. But then he laid the pistol down and leaned back and laughed. "Mackenzie, Mackenzie," he said. "What am I going to do with you? You've just made my point. I need a man with spirit, God damn it, who's not afraid to talk back to me."

He pointed a finger at Mackenzie. "In point of fact you're not entirely wrong. America *had* gone down the wrong road in many ways; I'm working on a book in which I—" He pulled himself back. "Permissiveness, weakened moral fiber, disrespect for authority, yes, perhaps the America we loved and served *did* almost die. But we're going to bring it back, Mackenzie. We'll restore the land of the free—"

"By enslaving the people at gunpoint for your chain gang?" Mackenzie said sardonically.

"Now you see, there you go again." Decker shook his finger almost playfully. "Slavery indeed. Volunteers, Mackenzie. At least I assume our civilian workers are helping us voluntarily. As loyal Americans, I assume they're willing and even honored to have the opportunity to serve their country, in whatever capacity and despite whatever sacrifices. If any of them feel otherwise, of course," he said, "then as traitors they deserve to pay for their disloyalty with a little honest labor."

He leaned back, still smiling. "On the other hand," he said more seriously, "I won't argue with your term or with the idea. Slavery is an ancient and valuable human institution, Mackenzie. It formed the basis for all the greatest civilizations—Rome, Egypt, China, even the Aztecs—and I've never agreed that we in the United States were wise to abandon it; we certainly let ourselves in for a lot of future trouble, turning all those Negroes loose to collect in the cities and breed. . . . Of course the mistake was in bringing in numbers of a genetically inferior race to begin with; it would have been wiser to employ slaves from backward European countries. The Russians, for example, would have been happy to sell the American colonists any number of Polish peasants."

"Interesting theory," Mackenzie observed. He looked strangely tired.

"Yes, well, it's theory now, but who knows, when we rebuild America we'll have a chance to correct a great many past mistakes, won't we?"

He stood up, leaning across the desk, looking into Mackenzie's eyes. "You have no idea," he said earnestly, "just how big this is, this mission we're on. You have no idea of the opportunity I'm offering you. In a very short time, Mackenzie, it is going to be in our power to change the history of the world."

Mackenzie nodded slowly. "In that case, General, if it's all the same to you, why don't you just go on and change it without me? Somehow it doesn't sound like the right career move for me this year."

Decker turned his back on Mackenzie, struggling for control. Why did he let this fool get to him like this? After a choked pause he said, "Very well. I never force men to serve in the Army. Certainly not as officers. I want only those who believe in the holiness of our cause and our mission."

He turned back to face Mackenzie, finding himself looking up at the taller man. For the first time in years he felt *short*.

"Still," he said almost sweetly, "we don't want to waste your valuable physical assets in Bob's kitchen. Too much real work needing to be done, Mackenzie—can't have a strong man washing dishes like a girl. Back to the track gang, starting next stop. I'll tell them to make sure you're, um, fully utilized."

When Mackenzie was gone Decker sat at his desk for a little while, the anger inside him still boiling, but the control slowly coming back. At last he rapped on his desk and called, "Hooten!"

The orderly came quickly in from his little cubicle. "Sir?"

"You heard, Hooten?"

"Yes, sir," Hooten said cautiously.

"Learn from this, Hooten." Decker leaned far back and swiveled his chair around to gaze at the light coming through the observation dome. "Everyone has some use in the Big Picture."

He gestured broadly, his back to Hooten. "That man. A traitor, a subversive, possibly even a closet Red of some sort. Yet he will be made to serve the cause, even as you or I."

"Yes, sir?" Hooten sounded slightly confused.

"We've come a long way, Hooten. Haven't had all that much fighting in the last few days, just hours of rather slow travel. The troops are getting bored and slack. A little inspiration and motivation is in order. Haven't had a formal execution since Bakersfield. That man Mackenzie," he said cheerfully, swinging back around, "ought to do nicely."

He smiled at Hooten. "Not now, of course. Can't spare the time till we get to the objective, and we might need all our labor force until then anyway. Meanwhile, pass the word that Mr. Mackenzie is to be made to work very hard for his keep."

Hovik said, "You *what*?"

Billy Blackhorse said, "Well, you said you wanted some dynamite."

7

Squinting through the old Nikon binoculars, turning the knurled focus knob slightly, Hovik said, "Well, I am a son of a bitch. There really *is* a train."

Beside him Joe Jack Mad Bull looked smug. "Hey, I been telling you. There it is, bigger than shit. Somebody got himself a real choo-choo for Christmas."

They lay side by side at the crest of a sharp rocky ridge overlooking the tracks. Stone outcrops and scraggly bushes concealed them, but they were in no real danger of being seen anyway; the train was a quarter-mile or more away and they had the sun at their backs. It was early afternoon.

"They been working on that bridge since around noon," Joe Jack said. "They were already stopped and had the work crew out when I saw them first, and in the time it took me to go get you and bring you back here, it looks like they still haven't got it fixed."

"Wonder where the hell they're going," Hovik said absently. "That main line goes up through the mountains and I think it finally turns east and wanders off through north Nevada—Winnemucca or something—but there's all kind of branch lines up in these mountains, too, mining stuff mostly. Can't think what they'd want with any of it, though."

"Maybe they're just jacking around."

"Bullshit. Look at that thing. That ain't just a train, man. In fact the train part is just something to carry weapons and armor. Whoever the hell that is down there, it ain't Casey Jones." Hovik swung the binoculars and whistled. "God *damn*, that's a MacArthur tank, last model they made, we had them in Iraq. Somebody down there believes in going loaded for bear."

"You don't suppose it's the military?" Joe Jack sounded dubious. "I mean the real military. You know, like maybe somewhere there's some part of the government that survived all that business ten years ago and now they're trying to pull it all back together?"

"I doubt it. Although from the flag and the bird painted on the engines, I figure these dudes *think* they're the government, or got plans to set up in the government business." Hovik shook his head. "Long as they do it a long way from here, that's not our problem."

He lowered the binoculars and looked at Joe Jack. "Thanks for showing me this thing, I wouldn't have wanted to miss it. Still and all, I don't really see where it's got much to do with us, do you? Assuming they get that bridge fixed and move on without bothering anybody on our turf."

"Yeah, you're right. At least about it being somebody else's problem—and from the looks of that work crew and the guys pointing guns at them, I'd say this bunch has *been* somebody's problem, somewhere—but, well, you gotta admit the possibilities are there if we want to go for them."

Hovik scowled. "God damn it, Joe Jack, I knew you'd come up with something crazy. You go fucking with those people down there, they'll hand you your ass in a shot glass, and then they'll come make trouble for the rest of us."

"Yeah, but think of the stuff they've got to have on that train—ammo, gas, maybe medical supplies—"

"We already got enough ammo to fight a war, we got about as much medical stuff as any of us knows how to use, and as for gas that thing runs on diesel and so does that old Kraut truck they're using for a track sniffer. Shit," he said, "I know what's got your dick in an uproar. You want to go steal something off those bastards just so you can be the brave Cheyenne warrior again. Get the juice going, feel that rush . . . Hell, you think I don't know? You think I didn't think of the same thing when I saw that train?"

"Actually," Joe Jack confessed, "I was sort of hoping—"

"Sure. Let's face it, guys like us, we ain't really cut out for this life we're into these days—we don't make real great homesteaders. But there's people depending on us," Hovik said, sounding as if he were trying to convince himself. "I mean, we both got families—Christ, who am I talking to, you and your three wives—and you know, we go playing games with whoever that is down there, get ourselves killed, who's gonna take over running that collection of refugees and misfits back at camp? Billy Blackhorse?"

"Okay, okay." Joe Jack sighed. "Tell you the truth, though, what I had in mind was to take some of the younger guys down there when it gets dark, if they haven't got it fixed by then, and let *them* get a little experience. Do them good."

"Oh, my bleeding ass. Now I get it. This is one of your Indian numbers, right? Give the young braves a chance to earn honors stealing ponies from the soldiers. What were you gonna do, hand out eagle feathers afterward?"

"Yeah, yeah, I admit it, it was a half-assed idea." Joe

Jack rolled over on his back and stared at the sky. "But I need to come up with something. Young men do need a chance to prove themselves."

"Do it on some easier target, then." Hovik gave Joe Jack an odd look. "You still got this idea, don't you, that you're going to bring back the old ways. I been hearing all that drumming and hollering down at your end of the camp, and I couldn't believe it when you built that teepee. None of my business," he added hastily as Joe Jack started to speak. "Only it seems kind of impractical."

Joe Jack grinned, unoffended. He and Hovik went a long way back; they had been prisoners together. "Somebody's got to do it," he said. "And it's getting time to get serious about it. Look how we're living now, depending on leftovers from a world that's not gonna come back for God knows how long, if ever. What's everybody gonna do when the bullets are all gone? Or the last drop of gas? We ought to be trading around trying to get some horses, man, and somebody to teach us to ride them—hell, I can't ride a horse any more than you can—and learning how to make bows and arrows and stuff like that. Not because it's the Indian way, particularly, just because it's going to be the only way one of these days—maybe not for me or you, but for those kids you mentioned."

Hovik grunted. "Fuck the future," he said. "What did it ever do for us?"

"Yeah, but seriously. Some of these young guys—you take Tom Crosses River, or Larry Bushyhead, or Lone Hawk—"

"Lone Hawk, or Two Dogs Fucking or whatever he's calling himself now, is as white as I am. And Larry Bushyhead's only about an eighth Cherokee."

Joe Jack laughed. "Hell, Frank, that stuff doesn't matter any more. We're all Indians now, don't you know that? You too. We gotta give you a name—Bear Breaks Wind or something. Like it or not, you guys had your chance and from where I sit it looks like you blew it. Might as well join the tribe."

He sat up, looking back down the mountainside toward the long shape of the stopped train. "And that," he said, "is George Custer down there, if I know anything at all. Recognize the son of a bitch anywhere—and you watch, sooner or later we're gonna have to do something about him before he does something about us."

They walked back down the mountain together, headed for where they had hidden the dirt bikes. It was a long walk; they hadn't dared get close enough for the motors' sound to carry to the train.

"Actually," Hovik said suddenly, "you got one authentic Indian here with some real balls. Not a whole hell of a lot of sense, but he's got brass nuts, even if he does look like a geek."

"Billy Blackhorse?" Joe Jack looked surprised.

"Yeah. Remember I was bitching about wanting some dynamite? Kid comes in yesterday evening proud as shit. Seems he remembered that old mining operation up near where the railroad crosses the river on that big high bridge, you know? Figured they'd have had some dynamite around. And son of a bitch if he didn't go off up there by himself, poking around in those old mine workings—Christ, just going into an old mine by himself, that's so crazy I don't believe it. I know *I'd* have to want something awful bad to go in there alone."

"Did he find anything?"

"Found a whole stash of Du Pont, man, with caps and fuses and, from what he said, even one of those old hand-push exploder boxes. Of course he didn't know about dynamite, how it gets cranky and unstable when it's been lying around a long time—wonder he didn't blow the whole top of that mountain off and turn himself into Pawnee powder. I just about shit when he told me about it. Luckily he didn't try to carry any of the stuff out. There's a good chance it could have gone off just from touching it. Dynamite ain't like booze, man—it's more like women, it don't improve with age, it just gets dangerous as hell."

"Speaking of booze," Joe Jack said. "Did you happen to bring—"

"I got a bottle of Old Tarantula Piss in my saddlebag," Hovik said. "Aged almost two whole weeks. Billy's getting better or else my standards are going to hell."

The bridge was repaired a couple of hours before sunset. Mackenzie heard the guards speculating that they might just stop here for the day, but then the bell sounded and they got back on the train.

He was glad enough to get back to his boxcar, where he could stretch out on the hard floor that suddenly felt very good. The work had been brutal; the guards had singled him out for the hardest jobs, the most frequent abuse. It was obvious they had been told to give him the full treatment. He was pretty sure he knew who had given the orders, and why.

Well, he thought, that's what you get for shooting off your mouth. Why didn't you take the little prick up on his offer, let him hand you a gun and a new pair of boots, and then take off? Maybe even shoot him before leaving. . . . But he knew that he would have been watched closely for a long time before Decker trusted him; in fact his chances of escape would have been lower, at least at first.

He was going to have to get on with it, though; he realized he had fallen into a dangerous passivity. He remembered Alice Santana's remarks about people staying with the train because it had become the only life they knew. In a way, he thought, he owed Decker a kind of gratitude for waking him up; he had felt, yesterday, a level of anger that he had not felt in a long time. The rush of rage had surprised him as much as it had no doubt surprised Decker; it had, he found, burned away the gray numbness that had held him since burying his wife.

He thought many times that day of Alice Santana. He wondered if he would see her again.

As it turned out, he saw her that night.

It was some time after midnight; it was a cloudy night and he could not see the stars that were his usual nighttime clock, but he had heard the sounds of the changing guard shifts. He was lying on the floor of the boxcar in his usual place by the door, slogging through a restless discontinuous sleep that was little better than no sleep at all; the aches and strains and bruises hurt too much for real rest, and he had long ago given up trying to find a position that gave him any relief.

He did at least have plenty of room to stretch out, for the townspeople in the boxcar had behaved as if he might be radioactive; ever since his return at gunpoint the previous evening, they had been at pains to keep their distance. It was unlikely they actually knew anything about his encounter with Decker; more probably, it was just their natural reaction—obviously this man had in some manner incurred the anger of the overlords, therefore it might be dangerous to be seen in his company. Mackenzie was too tired even to be angry at them.

He had dozed off again, and was having a confused disturbing dream in which Decker had appeared aboard a space shuttle and tried to take command, when he was awakened by a series of sharp jabs in the ribs. He rolled over and saw Alice Santana's head and shoulders silhouetted at the bottom of the doorway. His hand came down on a long thin stick with which she had apparently been poking at him through the bars.

She said in a barely audible whisper, "Be quiet."

He moved silently over to the door and put his face against the bars. She said into his ear, "You can reach the lock from inside, can't you? I'm not tall enough and there's nothing to stand on."

He took the ring of keys she pushed through the bars. The big brass lock hung on the boxcar's side just beyond the edge of the doorway, and it was hard to reach from inside, but after some groping he managed to get it twisted into an accessible position. Fumbling in the darkness, afraid to make any sound, he tried three keys—there was a really bad moment when one went partway in and then stuck briefly—before finding the right one.

The iron-barred door made a small grating sound as he slid it back a foot or so, just enough to let him squeeze through. As he jumped to the ground he wondered if any of the people inside would follow him, but no one did; and then it passed through his mind that some idiot eager to curry favor might call out an alarm, but nobody did that either.

Alice stood beside the boxcar holding some sort of sack in one hand. "Come on," she said unnecessarily.

He glanced up and down the train, looking for guards, but he could see no one. Actually, he realized, he couldn't see much at all; the night was really dark and a light misting rain was starting to fall. He followed Alice's fast-sliding shadow back along the length of the train, still fighting to free his mind of the remnants of sleep. Everything felt unreal; he half expected to wake up and find himself back in the boxcar.

He caught Alice's arm and motioned with his left hand that they should head away from the train, toward the nearby line of forest and up the mountainside. Before she could react, however, a man stepped out from between two cars, holding a rifle in one hand and fastening his fly with the other.

Mackenzie's reaction was altogether instinctive; his hands moved much faster than his fatigue-dulled brain. The guard's mouth opened in amazement, but before a sound could get clear of his throat Mackenzie's hand was over his face, palm covering his mouth, and he was being hurled backward at great speed. The back of his head hit the armored side of the car behind him, very hard. There was a sound like a cantelope being dropped on a cement sidewalk, but it was not a sound that would carry far.

Mackenzie eased the dead man to the ground, taking the rifle from his hand and passing it to Alice. Quickly he took the man's square-billed cloth cap and, ignoring the wet spot in back, jammed it onto his own slightly larger head. The loose camouflage jacket came off easily; it was big enough that he simply put it on over the shirt he already wore. Taking the rifle back from Alice, he gestured for her to walk ahead of him. If anyone saw them now, they would be taken for a trooper and his voluntary-or-not companion of the evening.

Either it worked, or no one saw them to begin with; there was no outcry behind them as they climbed down the embankment and crossed the open ground and entered the solid darkness of the forest. There were more troopers out here somewhere, he knew, guarding the perimeter, but they would be under the trees cursing the steadily increasing rain. At any rate no one appeared to stop the runaways as they began to climb through the dripping forest toward the invisible ridge line high above the railroad.

When they were far enough up the mountainside to talk safely Mackenzie said, "Why?" His burning lungs seemed to prefer one-word questions.

Alice grabbed a sapling and pulled herself up beside him. "Decker," she panted, "gonna kill you. Found out today."

"What?" He stopped and leaned against a tree. "You sure?"

He could not really see her in the rainy darkness, but he could hear her fighting for breath. The slope was very steep here and the ground was slick and soft from the rain; rocks that seemed to offer solid footing turned and slid underfoot. Mackenzie looked upward, hoping they were getting close to the crest, but he could see nothing that way either.

Alice said with difficulty, "Mary, waits on the officers. Heard it all. Decker said, soon as we get to . . . objective, gonna make 'xample." She took several deep shuddering breaths. "Trial. Firing squad. Encourage the others," she finished, and began coughing deep in her throat. "Shit," she added hoarsely.

It did not really surprise him, certainly not nearly as much as the fact that she had decided to help him escape. About to begin climbing again, he paused. "How'd you get the key?"

"Huh. Sergeant of the Guard, been after me a long time. Whispered to him at supper, come take me out after guard change." Alice coughed again. "Promised him a blow job. Got his knife when he dropped his pants. Cut his throat."

Even through her labored speech, the last was said with a calm casualness that lifted the hair on Mackenzie's neck. She might have been observing that it had been raining, or telling him she had bought the key at a sale.

He said, "Thanks."

She did not bother to respond to that at all.

By the time they reached the crest the rain was coming down in great soaking columns, plunging right through the thick evergreen tops above them, the big drops drumming painfully on their heads and bodies. Have to get out of this before long, Mackenzie thought dazedly, no use escaping a firing squad to die of hypothermia. But they were still too close to the train to stop; it was unlikely that Decker would mount a major search effort, given the improbability of success under these conditions, but with two of his men dead he would almost have to make at least some attempt. Whether he would send out trackers and search parties in the morning was another question; he would have to balance his desire to punish the runaways against the urgency of his need to move on to the mysterious "objective," and Mackenzie had no idea which way that might go. With a borderline psychotic like Decker anything was possible. . . .

Stumbling down the easier far slope—they had climbed, it seemed, not the entire mountain but only a kind of shoulder—they emerged suddenly onto an old gravel road that wound off into the darkness. It was an obvious route if they were pursued, but it was far faster going, and they splashed along at a good rate, glad to be out of the foot-tangling, face-lashing undergrowth.

Both of them were shivering violently by the time they came upon the old log house. It sat back off the road among the trees, and they almost missed it in the darkness and the rain. It was obviously deserted; even in this murk they could see that the roof was partly caved in.

"Can we?" Alice said through chattering teeth. "You think we've gone far enough to be safe?"

"If they just make a short sweep and say the hell with it, yes. If they stick around tomorrow and make an all-out effort—if Decker says, by God, we're not going anywhere till those traitors are caught—then there's no way we'll get far enough to be completely safe, even if we walk all night." He started toward the ruined cabin. "I just hope there's enough left of this thing to give us some protection."

The door already stood partway open, hanging on one hinge. Mackenzie threw a couple of rocks in just in case a large animal was already using the place, but nothing moved. After a moment he went cautiously inside, hearing Alice behind him coughing and cursing.

A dim gray patch showed through the hole in the roof; otherwise everything was absolutely black. They felt their way cautiously along the wall and, groping with nervous hands and feet, found an area of fairly intact floor large enough to let them sit with legs outstretched, backs to the wall.

"We'll have to stay put," Mackenzie said, "and not go moving around in here before daybreak. This floor's rotten —you could break a leg going through it."

Alice was fumbling in the sack she carried. "Hope this stuff's not too wet," she muttered. "I wrapped it up in this piece of plastic out of the kitchen. . . . here, take this."

She had brought a couple of blankets, a little food—leavings from the last meal of the day, wrapped in a bit of cloth, cold but still edible—and the knife she had taken from the Sergeant of the Guard. Mackenzie had the rifle he had taken from the man he had killed, but no ammunition except what the magazine held. Not much, he thought, to try to survive in this wild country, but people had managed with less. And the blankets, at least, were utterly wonderful just now.

"You're really something, you know?" he said as she pressed against him under the blankets. She was still shivering, but not quite so hard.

"I'm something, all right." She tugged at the blanket and squirmed into a different position. "I'm out of my damn mind, is what I am. Running around in the woods in the rain, probably gonna get myself shot or worse, just for some crazy Belicana son of a bitch who didn't have any more sense than to piss Decker off. I don't know why I thought *I* was supposed to be the one to save your ass. Hell, you're an old man, too."

"So why did you do it?" He held her to him, feeling his own shivering subside.

"Damn if I know," she said sleepily. "Seemed like a good idea at the time, like they say. Quit hogging the blanket."

The rain stopped a little before daybreak. As the first traces of dawn began to show through the hole in the roof, they got stiffly to their feet and stumbled out into the pale half-light, clumsy and stupid with fatigue. Listening, they could hear no sounds of search activity, but that proved nothing.

"Let's get moving," Mackenzie said uneasily.

They walked on along the gravel road, the wet mud sticking to their soles. Mackenzie had become disoriented during the night; he was not certain which way they should be going.

Until they had put some miles between themselves and the railroad, though, it hardly seemed to matter.

Then, as the clouds overhead began to break up and the sunlight at last came through the treetops, they both heard it, farther away than they had expected, but unmistakable and entirely glorious: the throb and rumble of the train pulling slowly away, gathering speed as it grew more distant. For a long time they could still hear the sound coming over the mountains until at last that too was gone.

They both exhaled, looked at each other, and burst into half-demented laughter.

Later, about midmorning, they were still walking down the dirt road when they became aware of another sound, a strange whirring and clanking coming from just up the road. As they stood, about to take to the bushes, a couple of figures on bicycles came slowly around the bend: lean, dark-skinned, long-haired young men, mounted on a pair of really decrepit bikes that bounced and rattled as the riders tried to dodge the puddles and potholes. Both of the cyclists carried rifles slung over their backs.

Alice said, "Jesus. What now?"

Seeing Mackenzie and Alice, the bicyclists braked quickly, the nearer one almost losing it as his back tire slid on the still-wet road. They glanced at each other nervously and dismounted, dropping the bikes, fingering the slings of their rifles, which Mackenzie saw now were only .22's.

Moving very deliberately, looking steadily at the cyclists' faces, Mackenzie slung his own M16 over his shoulder and then held his hands out away from his sides, palms down.

After a long pause the nearest man—he was not much more than a teenage boy, Mackenzie realized, perhaps in his early twenties—came slowly toward them on foot, looking distinctly edgy. He had a feather stuck in his long hair. Besides that he wore only a pair of jeans, faded almost white and hacked off at the knees, and flopping-ragged tennis shoes. The rifle across his back, on the other hand, looked extremely clean and well-cared-for. His friend, who wore full-length jeans and some sort of leather vest, had moved discreetly to one side of the road and was holding his rifle casually across his chest.

Alice Santana said, "Hi. You guys live around here?"

The kid seemed to notice Alice for the first time. His face began to change expression very rapidly. As he opened his mouth Alice said suddenly, "Hey, you're a skin, right? I'm Navajo myself."

The bicycle rider appeared to swallow a couple of times. "Yeah," he said finally. "My name's Tom Crosses River. Who *are* you people, anyway?"

General James M. Decker said to the men who stood in front of his desk, "So. An unarmed civilian laborer and a girl from the kitchen crew break out of their locked cars, murder two of our men—men who were supposedly on duty, I'd remind everyone—and desert, and what happens?"

He glared at them. "Very little happens, it would appear. Nobody even discovers the bodies for a ridiculously long time, and needless to say," he said with heavy sarcasm, "they've passed right through our perimeter without attracting any notice, because our tough heroic fighting men are huddled under the trees with their ponchos over their heads, afraid of a little rain. And *then*, when we finally do wake up and start to react, we flounder about the countryside for a couple of hours, up and down the hillside in the rain, and all we've got to show for it in the end is one man with a broken leg from falling down in the dark. Marvelous," he said, looking over their heads. "Outstanding."

Actually he was using some license in his use of the word "we," since he himself had remained in his car throughout the search effort; but then it wasn't the business of a general officer to go sliding and slopping around in the muck like an infantryman. Anyway, he hadn't really expected to catch the fugitives, not under the conditions and with the head start they'd had. But it had been necessary to make the effort, if only for morale—the two dead men, after all, had had friends; there had to be at least a token attempt to catch the killers— and, of course, in the interests of discipline, it was necessary now to make a show of anger at the lack of results.

After a pause one of the officers, a heavy-set man wearing twin silver bars on his collar, said hesitantly, "Sir, is there any further action you want us to take?"

"Yes, Captain Grimshaw, there is." Decker looked the man up and down. "In fact, since you were in charge of the guard last night, I think you'd better take this as your personal assignment. . . . The prisoners in the boxcar from which that man escaped, the ones we picked up in that little town down south. None of them tried to escape, even though the door was left unlocked."

"That's right, sir." Grimshaw looked puzzled. "All accounted for."

"But on the other hand none of them called out or otherwise tried to give an alarm when Mackenzie took off. So they're not loyal followers of the cause, they're simply gutless cattle. No use even trying to recruit troops there, and we've got plenty of laborers—we can spare a few in the interests of restoring discipline and morale. Take care of it, Grimshaw."

"Sir?" Grimshaw was clearly at sea now. "Of what, sir?"

"The execution, God damn it," Decker said impatiently. "When we stop this evening. Or when we reach the objective, whichever comes first. Pick, oh, let's say ten of them at random—better make that all males, the men don't like to shoot women what with the chronic shortage on campaign—and shoot them. Do it five at a time, that'll look impressive. Make sure everyone watches. Oh, and give the firing squad their pick of the women from that car. Little positive reinforcement." He smiled at the officers. "Does wonders to tighten things up."

Hovik was down at the wellhouse, greasing the cranky old iron pump, when Joe Jack Mad Bull came striding down the gravel walk, an odd expression on his face.

"Better come up to the house, Hovik," he said. "Couple of new arrivals I think you're going to want to meet."

8

When Mackenzie was done talking there was a long moment while everyone looked at him and at each other. Finally Hovik said, "Damn if that isn't about as weird a story as I've heard in a long time."

"You think Decker's weird to hear about," Alice Santana said, "you ought to see the son of a bitch up close."

"I meant the train," Hovik said. "I worked a few months in the yards in Omaha when I was just a kid, before I joined the Corps—they finally found out I was faking my age and fired my ass—and I know a little bit about what had to be involved in putting that thing together and keeping it running. This guy Decker may be as crazy as you say, but he's not stupid."

Everyone was seated under the trees at the rough old picnic tables down by what had once been a softball field. Some of the young men had pushed tables together end to end, so there would be room for all; no one wanted to miss meeting the new people. In this remote area even a visit by a wandering trader was a major event; any strange faces that didn't have to be shot at were a welcome diversion. And these two had been aboard the fabulous train. . . .

"You've got that right," Mackenzie said to Hovik. "In fact now I think of it that's part of what makes the flaky bastard dangerous. You see the vain strutting horse's ass and you tend to forget that underneath it all, he's about as silly as a rattlesnake. Within the context of his own loony premises and goals, everything he does is extremely logical—and he's damned good, I'm afraid, at doing it."

He paused to sip from the drink in front of him. The homemade wine was beyond any doubt the worst he had ever drunk, heavily oxidized and thick with sediment; it might, he thought, represent a Missing Link between genuine wine and fruit juice that had gone bad. Still, it was best to be polite to his new hosts—who seemed, all in all, to be a truly remarkable group. He had a number of questions that he wanted to ask, but they seemed interested only in the train.

"You take that so-called Army of his," he went on. "There's no way more than a few of them could have had any real military background—hell, most of them were about Boy Scout age when all the real armies stopped marching permanently. I suppose he picked up some of them from paramilitary bands here and there, but that's a long way from the real thing. And yet," he said, "you watch them in action and it's obvious the man has somehow turned them into soldiers, or something disturbingly close to it."

"Yeah," Joe Jack agreed, "and that's even though he doesn't have any real government or authority behind him. I mean, they could all just tell him to kiss their ass, or shoot him in his, and who'd do anything about it? And yet even I've seen enough to know they do what he says. Guy's got to have something, whatever it is."

Hovik was studying Mackenzie. Not much there at first glance, but a tough son of a bitch, Hovik guessed, when the deal went down. Have to be, just to have made it here at all. Hovik said, "You sound like you got some military experience of your own. Army?"

Mackenzie said, "Marines." He gestured at the tattooed emblem on Hovik's massive right shoulder. "Like you."

Across the table Judith put her head down in her arms, knowing a sinking despair. Oh God, she thought, just what we needed. Somebody to play Old Marines with Hovik, just when he was getting over all that crap. Now we'll get to hear it all again, the same as the last time we had an ex-jarhead around the place, every time they get into the booze or the grass. From the Halls of Montezuma. Gung ho. And then Chesty Puller said we got Chinese in front of us, Chinese in back of us, Chinese in every direction, by God the sonsabitches won't get away this time. Semper fi. Why, God, why?

But Hovik merely grinned and said, "No shit? Officer?"

"Yes." Mackenzie met his eyes. "Is that a problem for you?"

"Oh, hell, no, not any more. A long time ago it would of been . . . never mind, we can swap war stories later on when we got nothing better to do. Right now it don't matter if you were the Commanding Officer at Portsmouth Naval Prison —which you weren't, as I recall, at least when they had me there. Let's get back to this God-damned train."

"Yeah, right, the train," Joe Jack agreed. "What we want to know is where the hell are they going with that thing, and why? We been trying to figure out what they're up to and drawing a blank all the way."

Mackenzie nodded thoughtfully. "I wish I could answer

the question for you. I've spent a good deal of time kicking it around myself, and I don't have much more than you do."

He drank more of the terrible wine. Actually it seemed to improve slightly after the first few sips. Or, more likely, his taste buds had simply died of massive shock.

"All I really know," he said, "is that Decker keeps talking about some great 'objective' that seems to be the whole point of this expedition into northern California. Obviously it's somewhere to the north of here, but I don't know how far. Alice?"

Down at the end of the table Alice Santana was having fun watching Billy Blackhorse watching her. His eyes were already beginning to glaze over and while his mouth wasn't actually hanging open, it wasn't entirely closed either. She had decided to wait a little longer and then turn her head and smile at him and watch him come completely unwrapped. What kind of smile, sweet or bedroom? Actually he was kind of cute in a goofy sort of way. Might be fun to—

"Alice," Mackenzie said again, louder, and she turned. "What?"

"You ever hear anything about how much farther it was supposed to be? You know, Decker's mysterious objective?"

She thought. "Mary heard him say something yesterday," she said, "about how one more day's run ought to get them there if they didn't hit any major blocks. That was right after he said that stuff about having you shot when they got there," she said to Mackenzie. "That's why I figured I better not wait around about springing you."

"A day's run," Hovik repeated. "What would that be, you figure?"

"It's almost meaningless," Mackenzie said, "given the

variables involved—track condition, grades now they're in the mountains. More if they stay on the main line, a lot less if they have to turn off onto one of those mountain branch lines. Not as much as you'd think, anyway—that train is surprisingly slow. The engines sound pretty rough to me, and I don't think the rolling stock is in very good condition."

"That don't surprise me," Hovik nodded. "Like I say, it's a wonder they got the thing running at all."

Joe Jack looked at Mackenzie. "Don't tell me you used to be a railroad engineer," he said drily.

"No, I was an astronaut. Anyway," he said as everybody laughed, "evidently Decker expected to get there some time today. And he means to come back the same way, I think, because I heard one of the officers tell the work-crew guards to make sure we did a solid job—they'd be using those tracks again before long, going the other way."

"Word was," Alice added, "we'd all be back in Arizona by the end of summer. Of course that coulda been bullshit."

"So," Hovik said, "what is it, this objective of his? You got any ideas?"

"Not a thing. Whatever it is, Decker believes it's going to change the course of history. I think he expects to acquire some sort of decisive power that will make him the supreme military ruler in the West, and eventually in the whole United States."

Hovik and several other people whistled. A female voice said, "Woo."

"What this secret is, how it's supposed to work, I have no idea," Mackenzie went on. "You'd assume it must be something of a military nature, or at any rate something that could be used as a weapon, given Decker's orientation. On the other hand, what sort of weaponry could he hope to find in these mountains that he couldn't get in the Southwest? By the military standards of this time and place, he's already the man who has everything."

"The way you describe this geek," Joe Jack observed, "it could be something really nutty. You know, like he thinks there's a cave with a magic sword in it that makes him the king, or people from outer space who'll help him conquer the world, like that."

"The world's last supply of Pez candy," Judith put in. "In those little plastic dispensers with Tweety Bird or Daffy Duck on them. God damn it, I'd join his Army myself for a pack of Pez."

"Anyway," Mackenzie said, "once he gets his hands on whatever it is, he means to use his power to restore the United States as a nation—according, of course, to his own warped ideas. And I'll tell you, he's got some hair-raisers."

Abruptly Hovik stood up. "Hell," he said, "I don't really care what the son of a bitch is after or what he's going to do with it. I just wanted to make sure he's not going to be making trouble for us. Whatever it is, if it takes him a day to get there, it's not close enough we need to worry about it."

Mackenzie started to speak but Hovik cut him off. "Later, we'll talk more about it later. Right now you two come on up to the supply building and let's see if we can find some clothes to fit you. Stuff you got on, looks like it's about had it."

Mackenzie spent the afternoon wandering about the camp. No one seemed to mind; no one asked him where he was going or what he was looking at, or even spoke to him beyond casual greetings. Evidently he was free to do pretty much as he pleased.

Which seemed to be the general spirit of this odd little community; the place seemed to be very loosely run, if indeed it was being run at all in any formal sense. Obviously the big Czech, Hovik, functioned as a kind of leader, and the man called Joe Jack also seemed to exert considerable influence—yes, and that magnificent woman named Judith was clearly a person of stature too. But whether they held any sort of office or authority, or were simply held in general respect, Mackenzie had not been able to learn.

There were, by his best estimate, about twenty adults living at the old summer camp, with perhaps an equal number of children; it was hard to know just where to draw the line in some cases. Except for the smallest children, everyone seemed to work, sometimes very hard—there were extensive vegetable gardens and cornfields, evidently cultivated by hand labor; he saw no tractor and no animals bigger than goats—yet there was a relaxed, unstressed air about the workers, and the few gripes and curses he overheard sounded essentially good-natured.

Alice had disappeared, right after lunch, with a couple of young women—a long-legged redhead and a chubby, pregnant Indian, both gigglers: Joe Jack's "wives," someone had explained. Evidently the camp's make-your-own-rules attitude extended to marriage customs as well; Decker would have been appalled. . . .

Mackenzie sat in the shade on one of the picnic tables, watching a couple of very small and violent children who were playing in the grass nearby. That was a loose use of the term; their idea of "playing" would have been classed as attempted homicide in any other context. Their vocabulary was really impressive in some areas.

The little boy—Mackenzie was not entirely sure of this; both children wore ratty shorts and nothing else, and both had identical roughly hacked-off hair—was crawling about, pushing and pulling a toy train made from tin cans and pieces of unpainted wood, its cars linked together with bits of rawhide. The wheels appeared to be the brass heads of shotgun shells. Funny, Mackenzie reflected, how children would play with toys that represented things they had never seen in their own world. Kids in the urban slums of his own day had loved little plastic horses and farm animals, even though they had never been anywhere near a farm and probably never would. Well, there was at least one train running in this part of the world, though he hoped neither of these children ever got a look at it.

The little girl (?) had for some time been stalking the train operator, an alarmingly large rock held in both hands. Suddenly, with a wild screech, she hurled it clumsily at the back of his head. Mackenzie winced, but the rock missed by a foot, smashing instead into the coffee-can locomotive of the train.

The boy rose, murder in his eyes. "You thorry little thyitathh," he howled. "You buthted my choo-choo!" He glanced about, obviously looking for a weapon, as she began to run. Finding nothing, he pursued her empty-handed, screaming lisped curses and threats. A moment later they had disappeared around the corner of the nearest log building.

Behind Mackenzie Alice Santana said, "Cute, huh?"

He turned as she sat down beside him. "The kids, I mean," she said. "Hovik's, somebody told me."

"Somehow I'm not surprised."

"Oh, well, yeah, some of the women been telling me

stories about him. Seems he's an even badder dude than he looks like, but they say he's really a big old bear when you get to know him."

Mackenzie had met a big old bear about a year ago, in the woods near his cabin. It had attacked instantly and done its best to kill him, and it had soaked up the entire contents of his .30-30 rifle before collapsing at his feet. From what he had seen of Hovik so far, the comparison seemed apt but not encouraging.

Alice said, "Hey, Mac, I'm really sorry I took off on you like that." She put her hand on his knee. "Just, you know, been a long time since I been around any skins."

He nodded. "There seem to be quite a few Indians here."

"About half the people here are Indians or mixed-bloods, they say. Seems that guy Joe Jack went around, right after the Plague, rounding up young Indians who'd lost their families. Me, I think there's some of them bullshitting about how much Indian blood they got, but that's none of my business, is it? No Navajos, though."

He noticed she was wearing a blue-and-white bead necklace she had not had before. Her braids had been tied with new red ribbons. She looked happy.

She put her arm around his waist. "Listen," she said, "what I came to tell you, Judith wanted me to ask you up to their place for supper tonight. Kind of a private scene at their cabin, you know? I think they want to talk some more about Decker and the train." She made a face. "Beats me why. I'd just as soon forget that whole crazy business."

General James M. Decker, Commander in Chief of the Army of America, watched as the first five condemned prisoners were brought out and lined up against the side of the boxcar. A nice touch there, he thought; the bullet holes would serve as a constant reminder to the remaining prisoners.

The five men were walking clumsily, heads down, their posture spiritless and limp. One man, Decker saw with great disgust, had already wet himself; the dark spreading patch was visible from this far away.

"Wouldn't you think, Richie," he said under his breath, "that they'd at least have enough manhood to try to die well? Tell Captain Grimshaw to proceed."

There was a sudden flurry of hand signals and shouted orders. All along the railroad right of way, the assembled troopers came to a semblance of attention. The remaining prisoners merely continued to stand and stare.

Grimshaw barked an order and the members of the firing squad raised their rifles. One of the five men began sobbing loudly. "Oh, *God*," Decker muttered. "Cattle, Richie, nothing but cattle. No wonder there have to be people like me to tell them what to do."

The crash of the rifles drowned out his last couple of words. It was a long ragged volley, the guns on full automatic setting, which distressed Decker; he would have preferred the classic one-shot-per-man style, but the truth was that his men simply were not good enough shots for that. The five men collapsed slowly, jerking and twitching, to lie beside the bloodstained crossties.

The short redheaded Sergeant walked over and looked at the bodies and called out something to the Captain. Grimshaw strode up and looked down, nodded, and drew his pistol. There was a single shot. The last body stopped moving.

As the five bodies were dragged away and laid beside the other five that already lay on the hillside, Decker said to his orderly, "Well, Richie, time for my little talk to the troops."

He walked smartly across the gravel, stepping over the rails without seeming to look down, swagger stick tucked under his arm. For the occasion he had worn his varnished and polished helmet liner with the four stars across the front. It bounced slightly on his head, but he did not think it showed.

He mounted the big flat rock with the help of Corporal Hooten and, standing on top in the afternoon sunshine, faced the assembled Army of America.

"Remember this day," he said in a strong and ringing voice. "Remember this place. We are now at a crossroads of history. What we begin today decides the fate of the American nation for the next thousand years. . . ."

9

After dinner was over they all went into the long candlelit living room and found places to sit. Hovik said, "Let's have a drink. Not that weasel pee *we* make," he said to Judith. "The good stuff. Hell, we've got company."

Judith opened a cabinet and took out an earthenware jug. "Some people make this down in the valley country," Hovik told Mackenzie, "at this old monastery. I mean, they actually know what they're doing. I did them kind of a favor once."

The wine was very good, something dry and white, a little like Chablis. Mackenzie sipped appreciatively, thinking that these people knew how to live, at least in some ways. The food had been excellent, too, if simple: roasted grouse seasoned with wild herbs, various vegetables, and tortillalike bread made from ground corn. With a slight start he realized he could easily fall asleep in this chair. Better go easy on the wine.

Hovik cleared his throat a little self-consciously. "What we got here, Mackenzie," he said, "is kind of a difference of opinion. So we invited you over, figured we could kick it around some, see how you look at it."

"Right," Joe Jack said, stretching his feet out in front of him and folding his hands over his midsection. "If I can remember what we were supposed to talk about, after a meal like that . . . Judith, you're gonna make me do like a big snake, spend a month sleeping it off."

Joe Jack Mad Bull had come alone. Mackenzie wondered why none of his wives had been included, but no one had asked about them.

"See," the Cheyenne went on, "we got a bunch of young guys here, some of them about the age where their balls are bigger than their brains, you know? We talk too much about all this train stuff in front of them, they're liable to get some crazy ideas and go try something on their own. Thought we'd better keep this discussion private till we got our own thinking straightened out." He looked at Judith. "That's why I didn't bring the girls. Dorcas and Minnie would have been cool, but you know Bonnie, anything she hears gets spread all over camp."

From one of the other rooms came thumps and muffled yells. Judith said, "Shit. Go on without me, I've got to settle the little thugs down for the night."

"I'll go with you," Alice said suddenly. "I like your kids."

Judith shook her head. "You're a very sick young lady. Come on, then."

When the women had left the room Hovik said rather irritably, "Anyway, *as* I was trying to say before damn near everybody in the world butted in, we got this basic difference of opinion here over what we ought to do about this General of yours. My own idea, leave the son of a bitch as alone as we possibly can, don't rattle his cage, don't even let him find out there's anybody in the area, and hope he goes away as soon as possible."

He glanced at Joe Jack. "Then we got some people think the other way. Want to go find this Decker or Pecker or whatever, jerk his trigger and see if he's really loaded."

"That's not what I said," Joe Jack objected, "and you damn well know it. I just said maybe we ought to check things out a little more, see what these people are really up to. I don't like being blind and deaf, to say nothing of ignorant. We've got a whole new team just ran onto our field," he said, "and we don't even know what game they're playing."

"Yeah, but I still say, you go poking around wherever they've wound up, it's just gonna lead to trouble. Whatever he thinks he's got up there in the hills, he thinks enough of it he's not about to let strangers come sniffing around taking notes. Ah, hell." Hovik threw up his hands. "We've batted this back and forth a million times, we both keep saying the same things. Thought, maybe if we bring in somebody else. Anyway, you know more about this General and his act than we do."

Mackenzie said, "Christ, why drag me into this? I never even saw this place or met any of you before today." And, he added silently, I definitely don't need to get involved in your internal policy disputes. "What do the others think?" he asked, stalling. "Or have you asked?"

"I'll tell you what one of the others thinks," Judith said from the doorway. Alice was not with her. To Mackenzie she said, "If you ask me they ought to send that girl up there to deal with General Decker. Anybody who can get those two little cannibals to settle down and shut up is tough enough to handle any man alive."

She sat down on the couch beside Hovik. "Believe it or not, she volunteered to stay in there with the Gruesome Twosome while we talk. Said 'heavy stuff' bored her." She shuddered. "God, what guts."

Mackenzie said, "If you don't mind my asking, what *do* you think about this business?"

"About Decker and the train and what we ought to do?" She shook her head, smiling. "I'm damned if I know, Mackenzie. I see both sides and I've been going back and forth. God knows I've seen all the fighting and suffering I want to see for the rest of my life. We've got a pretty good life here; I'd prefer to keep it undisturbed."

She wound her braid around her forefinger, looking thoughtful. "On the other hand, from what you say, it may be that Decker's going to be a problem sooner or later no matter what we do now. In which case we ought to find out all we can before he gets any bigger or any closer."

"He's already too big for us to fuck with," Hovik said darkly, "and the best way to keep him from getting any closer is to leave him alone and let him go away."

They all looked at Mackenzie expectantly. He said hesitantly, "Well. To tell the truth I hadn't thought much about any of this—I'm still getting used to the idea of being free again. Give me a moment."

"Fill his glass up, Judith," Hovik said. "Man needs a little lube job there. And pass that jug over here afterwards."

Mackenzie swallowed and reflected. After a minute or so he said, "It seems to me the question turns around what Judith just said—how much trouble does Decker represent for the future? If he's going to remain nothing more than a traveling fascist warlord with a little extra firepower, Hovik's right: leave him alone and let him go away. He's got you outnumbered and outgunned all the way, and if he knew where you were and considered you a threat or even a nuisance, he could march a company up here from the railroad and blow you off this hilltop and your only chance of survival would be to scatter and run like hell."

Hovik was nodding. "What I been saying." Oddly, however, he did not seem entirely comfortable about it. "Man makes sense," he added without real enthusiasm.

"On the other hand," Mackenzie went on, "what if Decker isn't quite as crazy as everyone's been assuming? What if there really *is* something that's going to make him suddenly a lot more powerful—maybe not as much as he thinks, that's pretty hard to imagine, but at least too powerful to ignore?"

"You really think he could take over the country," Joe Jack said skeptically, "such as it is these days?" He frowned. "What am I saying? Shape things are in, how big a job would that be?"

Mackenzie said, "The whole country, no, as I say, that's too much for me to buy. But if he somehow acquires the means of augmenting his power even a fraction as much as he says, I'm not sure he couldn't at least set up some sort of crude little dictatorship somewhere in the West. At the very least he could make a lot of people miserable while he's trying—and the shock waves could easily reach this far."

"That's right," Joe Jack agreed. "Guy starts campaigning around the country, taking over towns and stuff, if nothing else there's gonna be a lot of refugees coming up into the mountains trying to get away from him. Or, like, that bunch down in Sacramento that attacked him down there—what if he whips them next time so bad the survivors have to haul ass, and they happen to haul it this way? We got to think about all this stuff."

Judith said to Mackenzie, "Just as a worst-case scenario, as they used to say, suppose he does manage to go all the way?"

"Then everybody's in trouble. Believe me, you think things were bad toward the end, the last government we had—"

"Yes," Judith said flatly. Her face had suddenly gone very cold. "Yes, we do think things were bad. Some of us had a very good look at just how bad they were. Secret arrests, concentration camps in the desert, oh, and you've got no idea what else."

"Uh huh," Joe Jack said, getting into it. "Air you couldn't breathe and rivers you could set fire to. Food rationing and people out of work everywhere you went. Guys getting drafted left and right for two different wars at the same time, no sense to either of them. Eight little, nine little, ten little Indians sleeping in one room in the LA ghetto and ten more out on the street wishing they could get in there with them. Oh, it was a real barrel of laughs in the good old days."

"Agreed," Mackenzie said, "but then you'll understand what I'm saying when I tell you that Decker's ideas are much, much worse. Hell, he told me so himself—he thinks the last government was too permissive, too *lenient*."

"Christ." Hovik looked a bit shaken at that. "He said that?"

"Among other things, he wants to bring back slavery—this time, I think, on an interracial basis."

"Huh. All right, you've made your point. We don't want this asshole running things and we don't even want him taking a major shot at it in this part of the country. We're together on that?" Hovik looked around as Joe Jack and Judith nodded.

"So then what the hell do we do? Pin on some badges and go arrest him?"

"Let's not get crazy about this," Judith said. "Hovik, I don't want you getting killed, either."

"Logical thing," Joe Jack argued, "like I said all along, let's go have a look. Find out where this supposed objective is, and what he's after. Even money it'll turn out to be something so nutty we don't have to worry about it. You know, like the lost Ark in that old movie. Then we'll all come home and have a drink and a good laugh."

"All right," Hovik said heavily. "I got a feeling it won't be anything even halfway funny, but maybe I'm wrong. Only thing, though—you can forget that 'we' shit."

"That's supposed to be my line, kimosavee. I figured—"

"You figured wrong. Hell, we can't both go sticking our noses into something like that—what if it goes bad, who's left here? Suppose our crowd does have to pull out in a hurry under attack, like this guy said. They'll have to have somebody who can take charge, somebody they'll follow without hesitation, and right now that's you or it's me, it ain't anybody else around here."

Joe Jack looked unhappy, but he said, "I guess you're right. But Jesus, Frank, you can't go up there by yourself."

"Actually I probably could," Hovik grinned, "but I didn't have it in mind."

He turned to Mackenzie. "How about it, Mac? You want to come along and see what your old buddies are up to?"

It was dark when Mackenzie and Alice left the big cabin and headed down the moon-white drive toward the quarters they had been given. Behind them Hovik called, "Get some sleep, Mac. I'll be coming for you early."

"You're going somewhere with Hovik?" Alice asked.

"Yes." He had already decided not to tell her the details; she did talk a good deal. "I'll tell you about it when we get back."

Down at the far end of the camp, on the old ball field, someone was beating a drum, a steady two-beat pattern: *boom-boom, boom-boom, boom-boom*. There were shouts and shrieks of laughter. "Some of the young ones," Alice said, "having a little blowout. Want to go?"

Mackenzie shook his head. "Hovik's right, I do need to get some sleep."

Voices rose in song to the beat of the drum:

"I'll see you all next summer at the Albuquerque
  powwow,
We'll dance the Forty-Nine again,
Ya hey ya ho yo hey. . . ."

Alice shifted uncomfortably from one foot to the other. "Well—you mind if I go, then? Like I said, been a long time."

"Go on." He touched her upper arm as she hesitated. "Really, it's all right. Go have a good time."

She ran off down the drive and disappeared into the darkness. Mackenzie stood staring after her for a moment and then he started walking again, head down, hands in pockets, feeling a sudden depression.

Judith appeared beside him so silently that he jumped slightly when she spoke. "Talk for a minute?" she said in a low voice.

She fell in beside him, laughing softly. "What's the matter,

Alice take off and leave you alone? Don't worry, she's just having a few laughs. She'll come back."

Mackenzie shrugged. "I don't have any hold on her," he said. "Hell, I'm old enough to be her father and then some."

"Oh, don't give up so easily. We had a little talk while we were putting the Spawn of Frankenstein to bed. You've got more there than you realize. Of course," she added, "I don't know what you want to do about it. . . . Mackenzie," she said, "don't get the wrong idea about Hovik. You're going to be taking off with him on a dangerous and difficult mission, it's important that you understand what's happening with him."

She turned and looked at his face. "You were telling the truth, weren't you, about being an astronaut? Everybody thought you were being sarcastic, but I saw your face. This is something you've done before—told people the truth because you know they won't believe you."

"It's true," he confessed. "Don't tell the others. Not yet, anyway."

"All right. I think I remember you," she said. "On TV or a magazine cover or something. It was a long time ago, wasn't it? What happened?"

"Politics," Mackenzie said. "I made a few incautious remarks here and there. The Administration decided I was politically unreliable. I was allowed to retire, more or less gracefully."

"Hm. Well, you probably picked up the impression that we had our problems with the late Administration too."

"I did."

"Hovik and Joe Jack," she said, "were political prisoners together—I know, I know, you can't picture Hovik as political, it's a long story and basically it was a mistake. I was involved in the Resistance. They escaped—well, as I say, it's all a long story and very complicated."

She stopped and faced him. "Mackenzie—no." She seemed to pull herself back from something she had been about to say. Taking a deep breath, she began again. "Let me just explain this much. In the final days, just before the —the Plague, we were in a big fight. An attack," she said, still seeming to talk around something she could not say. "On a, a secret government installation. Hovik planned and led the whole thing."

Mackenzie looked curiously at her. "And?" he said.

"In the end," she said with a strained note to her voice, "something . . . happened, never mind what. A great many people died, most of them innocent. It wasn't Hovik's fault, but still, he led the attack that was the cause of their deaths."

"I get the feeling," he said, "you're telling me only a tiny bit of the story."

"Yes. The whole truth—" She shook her head violently. "No, no, there's no way I can ever talk about that, to you or anyone else. I don't even have the right."

Mackenzie said, "So anyway, Hovik feels guilty now?"

"Not in any usual sense. It's been pretty much Hovik against the rest of the world since the day he was born; he might feel guilt if he thought he'd caused the death of someone he knew personally and cared about, but faceless strangers, no matter how many—no. But," she said, "he *is* a little gunshy when it comes to starting things that might get beyond his control."

"Ah!" Mackenzie said. "And that's why he's so reluctant to go after Decker."

"Right. He's no coward, Mackenzie. He carries weapons

and believe me, he doesn't hesitate to use them. It's just that he remembers what happened the last time he got involved in something over his head."

Down at the ball field the drum was still booming. The voices sang:

> "My darling said she loved me,
> But then she went and left me,
> That's when I started drinking,
> Ya hey ya ho yo hey. . . ."

"Go with him, Mackenzie," Judith said. "Look out for him, watch his back, don't let him risk too much. I can't even conceive of life without him."

She touched his arm. "Watch out for yourself, too."

In the dark cabin he lay awhile thinking, not trying very hard to sleep. It was very late before he finally slept. The drum was still beating.

Alice did not come in all night. He told himself it didn't matter, but it did.

10

In the last half-hour before dawn Hovik got up and dressed and walked down the drive to where the old green pickup truck sat parked under the trees. He raised the hood, wincing at the loud grating squeal, and tinkered briefly with the carburetor, draining the bowl and carefully dripping a little straight gasoline into the carb from a small bottle he took from under the seat.

The truck had, according to standard procedure, been parked facing down the steepest slope in camp. Hovik twisted a couple of wires together—there was no key—and released the brakes and let the old pickup roll. As it gathered speed he put it in gear and let in the clutch.

The engine bumped and popped, caught and lost it. Hovik cursed, clutched and declutched. Finally, just as the truck was beginning to lose forward motion completely, there was a rattle and a bang and the engine started, running raggedly at first, a couple of cylinders taking their time about getting in on it, but running all the same.

Hovik sighed, greatly relieved. The fuel they had to use

nowadays was heavily cut with home-distilled alcohol—in fact the truck's tank probably contained less than fifty percent genuine gasoline, and that not very good quality—and while it would run an engine after a fashion, it could be a son of a bitch to start. In wet weather it often soaked up water right out of the air.

He drove back up the gravel lane and parked in front of his cabin, leaving the engine idling and hoping it wouldn't quit on him before it got warm. Inside, he collected the things he had put beside the door last night: the packs, the bedrolls, the canteens, and the big plastic jug of water. He took it all out and tossed everything into the back of the truck.

Going back inside, he took a camouflage-patterned bush jacket and slipped it on, patting the big pockets to make sure he had the maps. Over the bush jacket he settled a standard military web belt, hung with his holstered .45 and his big Ka-Bar knife and a canvas pouch with a couple of loaded clips. He touched the black bandanna tied around his head and smiled grimly to himself in the dim light: at least that was one mistake he wouldn't be making again.

As he stood there, stowing various small items in his pockets and tightening the laces of his lug-soled boots, Judith appeared in the doorway. "On your way pretty soon, I suppose," she said in a voice still whispery from sleep.

He paused to look at her. She wore nothing but an old black tee-shirt that had been his. He thought of the last hour before sleep and his groin twitched in fond remembrance.

He said, "Hell, I probably won't be gone long enough to need half of this junk. Just figured, you know, since I got the truck and all, might as well take it in case we have to spend the night somewhere."

She said, "Be careful, Hovik."

He grinned. "You know what Joe Jack always says—if people were careful, wouldn't many of us be here."

He went over and put his arms around her, reaching down to pat her bottom. Really a nice one, too, he thought, what am I, crazy, leaving this woman to go off in the woods with another guy?

She wiggled slightly against him. "Is that a gun or are you just happy to see me? No, damn, it *is* a gun."

"I better get out of here while I still can." He disengaged and moved toward the door, picking up the M16 that leaned against the wall. It wasn't a weapon he particularly cared for, but he wasn't going out looking to shoot anybody; if he and Mackenzie had to fire their weapons at all, it would be defensive shooting, laying down as much fire as possible to allow them to get away—or, at the very worst, trying to take as many with them as they could. . . .

He jerked his mind back to the present. "Later," he said to Judith, and went out the door and walked down the road to get Mackenzie.

As they got into the cab a little later, slamming the dented doors, Hovik said, "I brought some more ammo for that sixteen you were carrying when you arrived. I guess I should of asked if you'd rather have some other kind of weapon."

"No, that's fine." Mackenzie rubbed his eyes. "I hope you've got this trip planned," he added as Hovik drove toward the gate. "You know this country better than I do."

Hovik lifted his shoulders slightly. "I got a few ideas. You get right down to it, there ain't all that many ways they could of gone. I mean, hell, this is a train we're talking about, not a bunch of guys on foot or riding horses—they can only go where there's a track, and in this country there's only so many places you can even run a track. Specially for a full-size road rig like that," he added, "instead of some narrow-gauge mining or logging setup."

Driving one-handed down the rutted mountain road, he dug the map out of his pocket and passed it to Mackenzie. "See," he said, "the main line follows the river pretty close through that stretch, because that's the easiest route through the mountains—goes right along the gorge in places, crosses the river a couple of times. I used to drive trucks up through here some, and the main highway follows pretty much the same route, got the railroad in sight a lot of the way. And I can't think of any place on the main line where there could be anything like what this guy's after."

He reached over and tapped the paper. "You can see, though, there's several branch lines running off into the mountains, and there's all kind of old mines and stuff up that way, where something could be hid."

While Mackenzie studied the map, Hovik steered the truck down the gravel road and, some time later, onto an old blacktop highway, its surface cracked and eroded, weeds and full-sized bushes sprouting freely through the ruined asphalt. It was not much smoother than the dirt, but the truck could at least go a little faster.

"Main highway, such as it is," Hovik said. "I hope Decker don't have anybody watching it."

The alcohol-gasoline mix had no power at all, even though the carburetor jets had been modified to burn it better. The old truck crept slowly up even moderate grades, coughing and threatening to stall. It ran fairly well on level stretches, however, and on long downhills it could actually move at a good clip. Hovik cranked down his window, enjoying the wind in his hair. "Hope they got wherever they were going and stopped," Hovik grunted. "If they're still moving we'll never catch them with this piece of shit."

"I don't know," Mackenzie said, looking at the speedometer. "I think we're still making better time than the train ever did."

The road swung left and crossed the river on a high-arching bridge. The river was a long way down, a silver streak at the bottom of a steep-sided gorge or canyon—Hovik wasn't sure of the difference, if there was one—and dotted with the white manes of rapids. Beyond the bridge the road climbed steeply, the truck wheezing desperately and moving at little more than walking speed. As the road at last leveled out to follow the curve of the mountainside, Hovik stopped the truck for a moment and pointed. "Look there."

Below them, the railroad tracks vaulted the river gorge on their own bridge, perhaps a mile upstream from the highway bridge. Great stone cliffs, eroded into strange and spectacular shapes, towered above the river on either side. From here the whole thing looked like an unusually well made model railroad layout; the track appeared no wider than a cigarette.

"Came across that bridge," Hovik reminisced, "long time ago, riding a freight, freezing my ass in a boxcar. I'd busted out of San Quentin a couple months before and you could say I had a good deal on my mind, but I still remember how the view blew me away. Sat there hanging my legs out that boxcar door, watching the river way down past my feet, then looking up at the cliffs and hoping to hell nothing came loose."

He glanced over at his passenger. Mackenzie, he saw, had fallen asleep.

"Cool son of a bitch," Hovik said to himself.

The truck grunted and hesitated when he started to pull away, and he cursed. Water in the fuel again, no getting away from it. He stepped on the clutch, raced the engine hard to clear the bowl, and shifted down for the next climb.

A good while later—the sun was getting high in the bright clear sky—Hovik braked to a stop, shook Mackenzie awake, and said, "Come on." Without waiting for a reply he got out and walked over to the railroad tracks.

They were down in another gorge, or another stretch of the same one, and the road came very close to the tracks here. Hovik squatted between the rails and studied the rusty surface of the steel. "I was right," he said to Mackenzie. "No train's been here in a hell of a long time. Look at that rust. Hell, look where that bunch of vines are growing right across the track."

"So they didn't come this way," Mackenzie said. "So what now?"

"So I just about know where they did go. There's not but one branch off this line between here and the bridge—hell, you got the river on one side all along that stretch, never more than a mile away, and big mountains on the other side, there's not but one place you *could* run a branch that would go anywhere." As they walked back to the truck he said, "I know where it is—we hunt up this way a good deal—but I don't know where it goes, you know? Never got around to checking it out. Never really expected to be stalking a God-damned train, here or anywhere else."

They got back into the truck, which was still idling. Hovik said, "Okay, so far it's been easy. Now you want to stay awake and hang on. Where we got to go, it gets pretty damn rough."

* * *

It was pretty damn rough and very damn rough and often unbelievably damn rough. Hovik drove along a series of badly eroded gravel roads and jeep tracks, gunning the underpowered vehicle hard as they splashed across shallow creeks, sliding the bald tires on washed-out fans of loose gravel and mud, a few times having to stop while they took the axes out of the back and cleared the way. There were gullies like trenches and potholes like bathtubs and they seemed to hit everything at the worst possible angle, even though Hovik drove slowly and wrestled constantly with the wheel.

"Glad we ain't hauling nitro," Hovik remarked. "Hey, remind me to tell you the story about Billy Blackhorse and the dynamite."

He glanced suddenly at Mackenzie, remembering something, thinking perhaps it had been a mistake to mention that last name; but Mackenzie did not react, and Hovik told himself the man couldn't possibly know. Early that morning, walking down to get the truck, Hovik had seen Alice Santana coming out of the trees beside the softball field. Billy Blackhorse had been with her, and his face had worn an expression that suggested he had finally understood something he'd been wondering about for a long time. . . .

The dirt road dipped down and crossed a set of rails. Hovik stopped the truck on the track and opened his door and leaned out, not bothering to get down. "Hell, yes," he said happily. "Been a train along here for sure. See all those little bushes growing up between the crossties, they've been busted down, and not all that long ago."

He slammed his door and looked at Mackenzie. "Assuming there ain't two different trains running around these parts—and if there are, I'm outta here—we're on the right trail now.

Christ," he said, relieved, "I can't believe it. I didn't really think I knew what the fuck I was talking about."

They rattled on up the old dirt road, climbing higher into the mountains, crossing and recrossing the rails a number of times. At last Hovik said, "Okay, I think we've about pushed our luck all we better. No telling how much farther we got to go, but they'll hear us coming in this thing a long time before we see them."

He slowed the truck, studying the road ahead. They had come to another crossing of the track. On the other side the road climbed sharply up a rise and turned off through the woods. Hovik gunned the truck up the grade as best it would go and, at the top, reversed off the road and backed carefully into the cover of the trees. He stopped the engine and looked at Mackenzie. "Here's where we get out and walk. Hope to God this thing starts when we come back, or we got one hell of a hike home."

As they shrugged into their light packs Hovik said, "Like in the Corps . . . officer, huh? How high'd you get? Get you a silver bar?"

"Silver leaf," Mackenzie said, adjusting a strap. "Lieutenant Colonel."

"You shitting me?" Hovik stared at him. "No, I guess not . . . Christ, though, you don't look that old. What were you, staff?"

"Aviation."

"Oh. Yeah, they did make faster rank. Son of a bitch." He picked up his rifle. "Well, Colonel, today you get to march with the enlisted men."

Walking back down the road toward the railroad track, Mackenzie said, "What's this problem you've got with officers? Or had? Maybe I need to know."

"Oh, no, it's got nothing to do with you. Or nowadays," Hovik said as they turned and began to walk up the track. "Something that happened a lot of years back, down in the marshes at the mouth of the Shatt al-Arab. Kid lieutenant, so green he was still farting Quantico food, made a stupid mistake. Got most of my squad killed. So I hit him a few times."

Mackenzie laughed. "How hard?"

"Too hard, I guess. They took him off to the hospital ship for surgery and they took me off to Portsmouth Naval Prison for a year and a Dee-Dee. Forget it," Hovik said. "Like I say, it don't matter any more."

They walked up the railroad, sometimes beside the track, sometimes between the rails, maintaining a hard pace, pausing occasionally to look and listen but taking no breaks. Hovik felt his leg muscles begin to tighten and hurt; he had thought he was in shape but evidently he'd been letting himself go a little. Mackenzie was keeping up without signs of strain.

They were in high country now, the ground getting rockier and dryer. Stands of tall trees covered the mountainsides, broken here and there by open meadows. The track was climbing steadily. "They didn't go very fast up here," Mackenzie said. "Not with those old diesels on this grade."

"Yeah, and you notice there's been a good many places where they had to stop and work on the track. Lighter rails on a branch line like this, wood ties, not a lot of ballast, just naturally got fucked up more than the main line. I thought this was awful short for a day's haul, but I can see why, now."

The tracks stretched on and on and the hours passed and the sun dipped toward the jagged horizon and still there was nothing. May have to stop somewhere for the night, Hovik thought, should have brought the bedrolls. . . .

But then, far ahead, where the track cut across a broad high meadow, there was something, a pattern to the shadows that were lengthening along the right of way—

Hovik said, "Hold it," and held up his hand. A moment later he was moving rapidly toward the nearby line of trees, motioning for Mackenzie to follow. He got the big binoculars out and studied the track ahead, his shoulder against a big pine. Mackenzie said, "What is it?"

"Switch. I can just barely make it out from here, but that's what it is. See that kind of a line going off across the open ground? Got to be a spur track." He lowered the glasses and looked at Mackenzie. "I think we just got somewhere, Colonel. Let's stay under cover as much as we can."

They moved quickly along, parallel to the track, keeping in the shadow of the forest. Coming out onto the meadow, they bent low and crossed the open ground at a near-run until they reached the track. Squatting beside the rails, Hovik studied the switch. The points had not been thrown. The spur track that curved off to the right was rusty and weed-grown. Hovik said, "Shit. I thought sure this was it . . . wait a minute."

He followed the spur rails as they swung across the meadow. Behind him Mackenzie said, "Where are we going? Even I can see this track hasn't been—"

"Ah." Hovik stopped and pointed at another switch, almost hidden by the tall grasses. Another pair of rails curved neatly off in the other direction. The scraped-shiny steel glinted in the afternoon sun. Beyond the Y, a single track ran straight toward a narrow saddle between mountains.

"Right. See, this here's a wye—"

"A what?"

"You know, like the letter Y. Only actually it's more of a triangle, I guess. They went on past that switch back there, then they *backed* onto these rails here—there'll be a third switch on up the line, that way—and up this spur. Then when they come back out, they use this one, the way we just came. That way," Hovik said, "they don't have to back up all the way to the main line."

Mackenzie nodded. "All right, I see it now. So they went up this side track or spur or whatever you call it, and presumably they're still up there, wherever it goes. What now?"

"We make like the bear that went over the mountain, and go see what we can see. Only we're a little smarter than the bear, so we get back into the trees and work our way around in a big circle till we can get a look at what's on the other side of that little pass. And right now let's get off this Goddamned meadow," Hovik said, glancing uneasily about him as he began to move. "I feel so fucking *exposed* out here. Like I'm unzipped or something."

A little less than an hour later, Hovik handed Mackenzie the binoculars and said, "Here. Have yourself a look and don't let the sun glance off those lenses. Then tell me what the hell's going on over there."

They lay in the deep shadow of the forest, well up on the side of a steep rocky ridge. Below them, strung out along a narrow curving valley that was almost a canyon, the armored train of the Army of America sat silent on the spur track. The locomotives faced outward, back the way the train had come; fifty yards or so in front of the lead diesel, the point buggy squatted at the bend of the track.

On the far side of the track rose the eroded and rocky slopes of a good-sized mountain. Several old buildings, evidently part of a long-abandoned mining operation, clung to the lower mountainside, their roofs fallen in, their walls black with rot. In the midst of the ruins, perhaps a quarter-mile up the mountainside from the railroad track, a great dark rectangle marked the mouth of a large tunnel. Or a cave, Hovik thought, but he decided it was too squared-off for that.

Men were swarming up and down the mountainside, mostly between the tunnel's mouth and the train. Some of them were carrying various objects, too distant to identify, and others appeared to be laboring to clear a trail or road up the slope to the tunnel, and a few were obviously standing guard about the area; but for the most part their activities added up to no recognizable pattern.

Mackenzie said, "Incredible." He was still looking through the binoculars.

"Hell, yes, it's incredible," Hovik agreed sourly. "Incredible we busted our asses all day long and this is all we got to show for it. All right, now we know where the bastards are, and where their God-damned objective is, but what good's that do us? The idea was to find out *what* they came up here for, and what they're liable to do with it." Hovik gestured toward the opposite slope. "Now we're here looking at them, and I can't see where we're any better off than we were when we got out of bed this morning."

"Morning my ass, that was the middle of the night." Mackenzie put down the binoculars and grinned at Hovik. "Well, we both know what we're going to have to do, and we knew before we came up here that we'd probably have to do it, so why all the pissing and moaning?"

Hovik glowered. Then, unwillingly, he started to laugh

under his breath. "Okay, Colonel, you got a point." He sat up and began taking off his pack. "Only we got to wait till after dark to do it, so meanwhile let's get some slack and have a snack. I'm so God-damned hungry I'm cross-eyed."

When darkness had fallen they made their way slowly and carefully down the hillside toward the track. Hovik led the way; following, Mackenzie was amazed at the silence and sureness of the big man's movements. For all his massive bulk, he seemed to glide from shadow to shadow without quite touching the ground.

But as they neared the train it became obvious that their stealth was wasted; the scene along the track and up the mountainside was so noisy and confused that they could have gotten away with anything less than a gunshot. Men shouted orders and questions and occasional curses, opened and closed boxcar doors, loaded heavy boxes and cases with much banging and thumping, and crunched up and down the scree-covered slope in heavy boots. Tools clattered and thumped against metal and wood, and somewhere on the train a small but badly muffled diesel engine was running—probably powering a generator, Mackenzie guessed, for bright lights had been strung along the track on poles, throwing the scene into garish contrasts of glare and shadow.

"Jesus," Hovik muttered. "It's a damn circus."

Up on the mountainside there was more ant-heap activity and more lights; the tunnel entrance was brightly lit both from without and within. Men trooped up and down the slope individually or in groups, uniformed troopers and parties of prisoners, while others shouted at them and gesticulated. Mostly, as best Mackenzie could see, they seemed to be engaged in carrying things from the tunnel entrance and loading them onto the train, but there were other operations going on at which he could not even guess.

He pointed; Hovik nodded. Together they eased beneath a boxcar and waited. When no one seemed to be near, Mackenzie slipped from under the car and quickly hoisted himself up and in, rolling into the darkness before standing up, hearing Hovik behind him doing the same. For a moment they stood listening, weapons ready, but there was no indication they had been observed.

Hovik said, "Better make this quick. This car ain't even half full. They could come with another load any minute."

The end of the car was stacked high with long wooden boxes. They seemed to be wired shut rather than nailed. "Should of brought wire cutters," Hovik muttered, reaching for his big knife. "Watch me nick the edge on this shit."

The soft wire broke easily. Hovik levered the lid up with his knife, stuck his hand inside and pawed through the packing material, and groped. "Holy shit," he whispered. "Good stuff in here."

Watching the doorway, Mackenzie said, "What is it? Guns?"

"Guns my crack. Some kind of a big hand-launched rocket, is what it feels like. We had something like this in Iraq. Blow the shit out of a tank, go right through the side of a concrete building, got its own little guidance system like a model airplane, and still light enough for a two-man team to handle. Or one strong guy if he has to. This is pretty much the same thing, I think." He closed the lid gently. "These bastards can have a lot of fun with this stuff."

Mackenzie thought it over. "Yes, but Decker didn't come

a thousand miles just to pick up some infantry hardware, even if there's a whole trainload of it in that mineshaft. My guess is that this is just gravy."

Hovik said, "Yeah, we need to—"

They both froze, then flattened against the boxcar wall, as boots sounded along the track outside and a voice near the door called, "In here?"

Another voice, farther away, answered in the negative. The boots moved on. Mackenzie slid the safety of his M16 back on.

Hovik said, "Let's look around some more. I don't like being trapped inside this thing. Found out all we're going to here, anyway. Wonder if we could just walk up the hill and have a look in the hole. We don't look too different from the others if we stay out of the light."

Mackenzie considered it. They both wore camouflage jackets—his own had in fact come from the trooper he had killed, though he had thrown the bloody cap away—and carried standard M16 rifles; nothing else in their outfits came even close to uniform, but then there was considerable variation in the troopers' equipment anyway. But Hovik's hair was much longer than was tolerated in the Army, and he himself might conceivably be recognized if the wrong person saw him—

"No," he said finally. "They've got that tunnel entrance lit up like a Las Vegas casino and probably twice as well guarded. We'd never get in alive." He moved toward the door. "Let's check a few other cars, look at some of this stuff they've got stacked beside the track, maybe we'll get lucky."

But as they jumped down and started toward the next car, a loud voice cried, "You two men!" A short angry man charged out from behind a stack of wooden boxes and confronted them, shaking a finger in their faces. "I saw you coming out of that boxcar! Been taking a little unauthorized break, right? Been hiding in there fucking off while the rest of us bust our butts?"

They stood in a deep patch of shadow, but Mackenzie could see the three stripes on the camouflaged sleeve. A couple of troopers had appeared now behind the Sergeant, holding rifles and looking tired.

"All right, God damn it." The Sergeant gestured with the rifle in his right hand. "You go with these two men. Detail of prisoners over there, you march them up the hill, I'll think about what to do with you later."

Mackenzie exchanged a quick glance with Hovik. It might be a way to get inside. "Right, Sarge," he muttered, and turned to go.

But the braying voice rose sharply behind them. "Holy Jesus Christ, look at that hair—how the hell you been getting away with that, soldier? And where'd you get that pistol and all that non-reg gear? Hold on there." The Sergeant's voice suddenly became hard and crisp. "Something's not right here—"

Mackenzie slid the M16's safety off, sensing Hovik beside him like a lion about to spring. Turn fast, shoot the three-striper, get the two troopers, and run for it—

The Sergeant's voice said calmly, "Don't try it, assholes. I got this sixteen set on full auto and I'll cut you both in half before you can move an inch. Drop the weapons or I drop you."

Mackenzie hesitated only a fraction of a second; there was no real choice. After a moment he heard Hovik's weapon hit the ground beside his. "Lose the pistol belt too," the Sergeant ordered. "Careful . . . now turn around, hands on your heads. Steiner, Willis!" The two troopers came closer, raising their rifles. "Cover these two . . . oh, my bleeding ass. I don't believe this."

The light where they stood was bad, but Mackenzie recognized the Sergeant now. It was the one called Red, the one who had captured him that first day.

"Shit fire," Red said delightedly. "Look, it's our old buddy. Where's your bicycle?" He looked at Hovik. "Damn, where'd you get this ugly old bastard?"

He gestured up the mountainside with his rifle. "Let's go, you poor fuckers. The Old Man's gonna be so happy to see you, he'll just shit."

General James M. Decker was indeed pleased to see them.

"Mr. Mackenzie." He beamed. "So good of you to return for a visit. And look, you've brought a friend. Gentlemen," he cried, "welcome to Project Ragnarok!"

11

"Ragnarok," Decker said cheerfully as they walked up the mountainside toward the tunnel entrance. "Do either of you gentlemen know what that means?"

And, when neither man answered, he went on: "Ragnarok, the Twilight of the Gods. The final destruction of the world in the war between the forces of light and darkness. The Norse version of the Apocalypse. Don't feel bad, gentlemen," he said, "I had to look it up myself. But you must admit, obscure or not, the name is appropriate to our situation."

Walking on either side of him and slightly to the rear, Hovik and Mackenzie remained silent. For one thing, it was a clumsy business climbing the steep loose-surfaced slope with bound hands, and took some concentration. For another, Decker was doing all the talking and obviously enjoying it. In fact he had hardly stopped talking since coming down from his private car to see the two prisoners. He was obviously in an advanced state of euphoria; his eyes fairly glowed and he gestured spasmodically as he talked.

I wonder, Mackenzie thought, if he's somehow found himself a supply of some kind of pills or nose powder. No, hell, he's just wired. And God knows he's got the right to bait us, after the idiotic way we walked into this thing. Whatever happens to us, we'll deserve it. . . .

The mine entrance was a brilliantly lit rectangle, much larger than it had looked from a distance, big as a two-lane highway tunnel in fact. Decker returned the salutes of the guards and said, "Carry on, men." To the four armed men who walked behind Hovik and Mackenzie, rifles at the ready, he said, "Come along, but if you have to fire those weapons in here, be careful of stray bullets, right? Remember what we've got down there."

The tunnel sloped downward from the entrance, not too steeply. A short way inside, piles of rubble and broken timbers had been pushed aside to leave an opening perhaps a dozen feet across. A group of ragged prisoners labored to enlarge the hole. Beyond the rubble, the tunnel opened up again, wide and lit by strong, regularly spaced lights along the rock walls.

"Ragnarok," Decker said once again as they walked down the tunnel. "You know, say what you like about the last government of this country—and I've said as much as most, Mackenzie, you know that—somebody, somewhere, was doing some real thinking. The nation was obviously in a state of decline—all the major nations of the world were on the decline, in fact—and it was clearly possible that everything might collapse suddenly, leading to anarchy and barbarism. A global war, natural catastrophes, civil rebellion: the possibilities had become almost endless."

Farther down the tunnel, a file of troopers moved aside to allow a loaded forklift to pass. "Oh, yes," Decker said as the forklift rolled past, "this is a remarkably well equipped installation, you'll see . . . as I was saying, it had become obvious that things could fall apart, drastically and very quickly, from one cause or another. So certain persons within certain government agencies came up with Project Ragnarok."

He looked at Hovik and Mackenzie. "You're both old enough to remember the so-called 'survivalists' who existed during our youth—private citizens preparing for some future catastrophe by stocking up on food, weapons, and other vital supplies, turning their basements into bunkers or building armed camps in remote places. Of course the government eventually had to put a stop to it, because you can't have private armies competing with the lawful authority of the state. Still, what you see here might be called the logical extension of the survivalist idea."

He spread his hands in a melodramatic gesture. "Project Ragnarok," he said, "was nothing less than a plan to establish a chain of secret bases in wilderness areas, where chosen groups of loyal personnel could take shelter during a general catastrophe, and from which they could later emerge to reestablish control and government authority. The occupants should, ideally, be able to survive anything short of an all-out global thermonuclear war, and should have enough firepower to cope with anything short of full-scale invasion by a major foreign power."

Mackenzie said, "Christ."

He had not meant to speak; the exclamation had been involuntary. But now Decker was looking expectantly at him, he said, "And that's what this is? A hole where a picked crew of devoted heel-clickers could huddle underground, like so many carrion beetles, waiting to pick over the carcass of the world?"

Decker halted and wheeled, hands on hips, to face his prisoners. Everybody stopped. A rifle barrel dug briefly into Mackenzie's back.

Decker said, "You know, Mackenzie, I'm starting to wonder about you. Knew you were some kind of Red, of course, but I had you pegged for just another misguided liberal type. Now, though, you turn up here, snooping around—I'm going to have to find out just who you really are and what you're up to. I think we're going to have a long conversation, say tomorrow." He smiled tightly. "One of the many useful features of this place is a small but well-equipped interrogation center."

He looked at Hovik. "And who might you be, anyway?"

"A local homesteader," Mackenzie put in quickly. "I met him after I escaped. He only came along with me out of curiosity, wanting to see your train. He's got nothing to do with any of this."

"So?" Decker looked Hovik up and down. "Doesn't look like a simple peasant to me. I'd wager this man has seen real combat in his day. Probably make a fine soldier in the Army of America." He shrugged. "Too bad, really. You've come here in bad company, big fellow. If you're with Mackenzie, I can't take a chance on you. Such a waste."

He stood for a moment as if expecting an answer, but Hovik did not respond, even with one of his usual grunts. Finally Decker turned and resumed walking down the tunnel. They were now getting deep into the interior of the mountain. Lateral tunnels opened on either side, leading off at varying angles, some lit like the main tunnel, most darkened.

"Some of this is a waste, too," Decker said regretfully. "Living quarters, for example, and life-support systems and supplies of concentrated food, to allow the occupants to live for extended periods without emerging at all—fully self-contained, like a spacecraft or a submarine. Even got a small gymnasium and sun lamps. All brilliantly planned and executed, but of course we have no use for any of it, except to add the supplies to our own."

Mackenzie said, "Which pretty much leaves the firepower part, doesn't it?" Keep Decker talking, he thought, after all this is what we came here to learn. "As your reason for this whole expedition, I mean."

"Exactly. You may have seen a few items as you were nosing around—those lovely antitank rockets, for example. Flame throwers, mortars, grenade-launchers, all sorts of explosives. Small-arms ammunition in bulk. Much more equipment than could have been used by the occupants of this place, but then the plan called for recruiting support, when the time came, from the surrounding country." He rubbed his chin. "To tell you the truth, I'm not sure we're going to be able to take everything, at least this time. There are several small motor vehicles—jeeps, trucks, a couple of tracked armored personnel carriers—that I'd like to have, but I don't think we've got space on the train, though at least we can take some of the gasoline supply."

Decker seemed to be getting off the track. Bait him a little, see what else he has to reveal. "That's your great objective?" Mackenzie said skeptically. "The big secret that was going to make you all-powerful—just a few carloads of infantry munitions? Pardon me if I have trouble seeing it."

Decker gave him a sharp sidelong stare. "Believe me, Mackenzie, the conventional weapons alone would have been well worth the trip. This isn't the whole Army of America, you know, merely a crack task force. There are others waiting, in Arizona and elsewhere, to be armed and led. With what I've told you about already, we could mount a serious offensive with excellent chances of success. For God's sake, Mackenzie, we live in a world in which fifty men with worn-out rifles and a handful of cartridges apiece can take over a city or terrorize an area a hundred miles across."

A smug triumphant look spread over his face. "*But*, Mackenzie, you're right, all the same. There's more, oh, you have no idea . . . up here," he said, pointing toward a side passage that slanted off to the right, its entrance guarded by a pair of armed troopers. "Now, by God, you'll see."

But there was nothing much to see in the big vaultlike chamber at the end of the passageway, nothing but a lot of big wooden packing cases perhaps twenty feet long and three feet to a side, painted olive-drab and marked with cryptic stenciled codes, stacked high and flanked by smaller crates on wooden pallets. Decker, however, was almost shaking with excitement and pride.

"Gentlemen," he said, "the Dominator."

When neither man reacted he said impatiently, "The *Dominator*, Mackenzie, surely you . . . no? But that's right, you were Marines, this is an Army baby. The M778 Dominator tactical missile, possibly the finest battlefield weapon ever developed. Launches from a simple rack that can be mounted on a truck—or a railroad car, aha!—or merely set up on the ground. Simple but accurate guidance system. Rugged, reliable, deliberately designed for ease of operation by relatively untrained soldiers—'user-friendly,' as they used to say—under any conditions. Range seventy-five to a hundred miles, more if you add the optional boosters. Warhead equivalent to a twelve-inch naval shell."

He smiled warmly at Mackenzie and Hovik. "But that's

merely the conventional high-explosive warhead, which is almost a waste of a fine missile. Because, you see, Dominator also takes its own specially designed *nuclear* warhead, which is a very different affair . . . that's right, gentlemen, I see I've got your full attention now."

Mackenzie found himself literally speechless; he could not have unlocked his throat at that moment if ordered at gunpoint to speak. Not, he thought numbly, that there was anything to say.

Decker made an over-the-shoulder gesture with his thumb. "The warheads are stored in another chamber, back that way," he said. "Nothing to see there—everything sealed in special shielded containers, of course, and kept partly disassembled for extra safety, though you'd be surprised how fast you can put one together and arm it. Also, besides the Dominator warheads, there's also a supply of small nuclear devices with time and remote-control fuse systems—intended, you see, for direct delivery. As for example a disguised commando team leaving one in a parked vehicle in a target area, or infiltrators placing a device against a strategically located dam. Some of these," he said, "are small enough to fit inside an ordinary suitcase, yet perfectly capable of taking out a small town or the downtown heart of a city."

He looked at their faces, obviously delighted with the effects he saw there. "*Now*, Mackenzie, who's crazy? A dozen nuclear-armed Dominators and an equal number of those pocket nukes, backed up by an ever-expanding Army with new and better hardware—still think I can't pull it off?"

A little while later, sitting behind a steel desk in what had evidently been intended as a command office, Decker said,

"Well, gentlemen, what did you think of—but wait, where are my manners?"

He beckoned to one of the quartet of troopers guarding the prisoners, spoke in an undertone to him. The man nodded and left the room. Decker said pleasantly, "If you're thinking of making some sort of play now that the odds are slightly better, I don't advise it. The remaining three are perfectly capable of killing you. And," he added in the same friendly voice, "please don't get any ideas of grabbing me and using me as a hostage. The men all have long-standing orders: in such a situation, shoot to kill immediately and don't worry about my safety."

Mackenzie said, "If you don't mind my asking a question . . ."

"Please feel free." Decker spread his hands. "Always a pleasure to talk with an intelligent man, even one who's chosen the other side."

"How did you find out about this place? Or rather about Project Ragnarok?"

"Ah. Odd business, that. Pure chance—or, if you like to think of it that way, the workings of Destiny or the hand of God or whatever. Some of my men," Decker said, "were checking out the wreckage of a crashed Air Force plane near what used to be Luke Air Force Base. Looking for anything that might be worth salvaging, you know—it was a small transport aircraft, I'm not sure of the make. Anyway, they found the body of a man in civilian clothing, with a large briefcase chained to his wrist. They chopped off his hand and brought the briefcase to me, and when we had opened it— not an easy job—and studied the documents inside, Project Ragnarok stood revealed. Or at least the basics," he amended. "Some of the codes were beyond our power to break. But, as you see, we learned enough to bring us here."

"I thought you said Ragnarok involved a whole chain of these places, all over the country. Weren't there any closer to your territory?"

Decker's mouth twisted. "Unfortunately, as best I've been able to learn, this is the only one that was ever completed. The pilot, I suppose, for the program. We found the place where one base was to be, in the mountains near Globe, but there was nothing but the empty system of tunnels." He sighed. "Well, if there are no more arsenals like this for us to use, at least there are also none to be used against us."

Mackenzie started to speak, but then the fourth soldier came back in, followed by a soft-faced young corporal—Hooten, Mackenzie remembered, Decker's orderly and all-around bootlicker. Hooten held a stainless-steel pot and a tray of plastic cups. A long-forgotten but unmistakable odor touched Mackenzie's nostrils.

"Ah, yes, thank you, Corporal Hooten." Decker smirked at Mackenzie and Hovik. "Coffee, gentlemen?"

Even Hovik had reacted, Mackenzie noticed; his nostrils had flared like an ape's. Decker, who was all too clearly enjoying himself, said, "You do drink coffee? Yes? Pour for our guests, Richie, there's a good lad. Sugar if you like, unfortunately no cream—oh, drink it straight, do you? Couple of real coffee drinkers, I see."

Mackenzie raised the steaming cup, holding it clumsily but tightly with bound hands. Even the smell of the steam was wonderful beyond belief.

"As I say," Decker smirked, "this place was well and truly stocked with all the amenities of life. Of course there's not really enough coffee to last long among so many—although you'd be surprised how many of the younger men never had the chance to acquire the taste—but it's a real morale-booster at a time when we're all having to work very hard."

He reached into a desk drawer. "As far as that goes— smoke?" He held up a pack of cigarettes.

Mackenzie shook his head. Hovik held up his bound hands and Decker tossed a single cigarette. "Give the man a light, Richie," he said to Hooten. "Those little paper matches, there. Never had the habit myself, never understood its appeal, but some of the older men went fairly wild when we found cases of these."

He watched as Hovik dragged hungrily on the cigarette. Making a face, he said to Mackenzie, "As I was saying, this seems to be the only Ragnarok base that was completed and stocked, and even this one turns out to be missing a few items I'd been counting on. In particular, there was supposed to be a sizable supply of chemical weapons—nerve gas and the like—with masks and protective gear, but apparently it was never delivered. Too bad. Think how we could have cleaned out that nest of human rats in Sacramento, for example, with a whiff of nerve gas."

"Shocking inefficiency," Mackenzie murmured, and gulped his coffee. It was terrible coffee—Bob, or whoever had made it, had obviously had no idea what he was doing —but it was still coffee, and it was glorious. He knew he should have refused it, should have refused to let Decker toy with him, but he didn't care.

"Oh, we'll make do with the nukes and the rest, we'll make do . . . by the way," Decker said, "I take it you've heard the stories—legends, I suppose you'd call them by now—about the origin of the Plague? That it was an artificially created virus produced in a government laboratory, accidentally released during a terrorist attack?"

"I've heard the rumors," Mackenzie said noncommittally. "Never put much credence in them."

"So?" Decker looked for a moment at the two men. Hovik had now withdrawn entirely within himself, his eyes hooded and unreadable. Decker shrugged and said, "Well, I felt much the same way myself, but now I'm not so sure. Studying the papers from that briefcase, and some other things we've come across here—I don't know, there might be something to it. A daring concept, anyway," he said admiringly. "Collect all your key people at places like this—immunized, of course—and release the virus. Let it thin out the excess population and wipe out the crowded countries of the so-called Third World, not to mention the Red enemies. Then afterwards the Ragnarok cadres—selected for intelligence, genetic soundness, and political reliability, of course—emerge and establish a new order."

"Rule by the rightful masters and none of this damned nonsense about democracy?" Mackenzie said.

"Exactly," Decker said quite seriously. "I don't know if it would have worked, but you have to admire that sort of vision. At any rate, they never got the chance to follow it up."

He stood up. "Well, this little conversation has been very enjoyable for me. However, the hour is late and we've got a long day tomorrow. Hell of a job," he said, "getting all this stuff down the mountain and onto the train, and of course you can't rush when you're handling things like Dominator warheads. Took us a good part of this morning just getting into the main tunnel—as you might have noticed, the mouth was blocked with rubble, to make the place look caved-in and abandoned. Then we had to get the generator plant going and so on."

He gestured toward the door. "Let's go, now. Time to show you to your quarters for the evening."

The interrogation room was a harshly lit chamber at the end of a short side tunnel. In the center were two long stainless-steel tables with gutters around the edges to catch body fluids. The ceiling was hung with ropes and pulleys. There was an ordinary dentist's chair, complete with drills, and a heavy wooden chair fitted with leather restraint straps. Various electrical devices were built into the walls. A Formica-topped table held such items as a soldering iron, a pair of long-nosed pliers, and a small propane torch. A coiled-up fire hose hung beside the door.

"Not a bad little setup here," Decker said conversationally, as the prisoners were brought in. "After all, as they prepared to go on the offensive, they'd have to be able to bring in prisoners for interrogation. And then, too, in an operation like this, you've always got to be prepared to stop subversion or the spread of disloyalty on the inside."

He looked around at the room and its appointments. "Yes, I was impressed when I saw all this, and I remember thinking what a pity it would never be used—no point taking any of this with us, we've got plenty of this sort of thing already, even on the train. But I see I was wrong. You'll have the honor of helping us get a little mileage out of this equipment after all. Well, it *was* your tax dollars that paid for it."

At the end of the interrogation room a pair of small cells had been cut out of the rock, side by side, perhaps six feet apart. The doors were solid steel, pierced with small view slits with sliding covers. At Decker's order the guards opened the doors and herded Hovik and Mackenzie into the cells.

"Leave their hands tied, sir?" one of the guards asked.

"Oh, yes, why not?" Decker smiled at Mackenzie as the door began to close. "I'm sure they'll get their hands free long before morning, but that will do no real harm, and it will give them something to do—in case," he added, "they have trouble sleeping. . . ."

12

When the door had clunked shut behind him Hovik backed slowly up and sat down on the narrow hard bed and, sitting very straight, closed his eyes. He sat there for a long time, breathing regularly, not moving; and then at last he opened his eyes, said "Shit," in an ordinary voice, and stood up and began to study his surroundings. Been a hell of a long time, he thought, but some things never seem to change.

The cell was smaller than the usual prison cell; he paced off roughly six by ten feet, most of that taken up by the steel-slatted bed bolted to the rock wall. There was a plastic bucket for a toilet. Overhead, recessed into the not very high ceiling and shielded by an arrangement of iron bars and metal mesh, a single bulb provided poor but adequate light. That was all.

He sat back down on the bed and applied himself to the cords that bound his wrists, all the while listening to the sounds that came through the door. He could hear fairly well; he guessed this was partly planned, a way of shaking the prisoner up by letting him hear what they were doing to the victim in the interrogation room.

He determined immediately that there was one guard on duty, sitting on some kind of metal chair or stool in the interrogation room, armed with a rifle—Hovik heard the buttplate thump the floor as the man sat down—and, from the sounds of his frequent small movements, a little restless on this job. At more or less regular intervals he was heard to get up and move toward the cell doors. The sliding panel would click open, first on Mackenzie's door, then Hovik's, and a pair of dark brown eyes, rather large, would peer in at the prisoner for a moment. During these checks Hovik always lay flat on his back on the bed, hands on his stomach, and looked up at the ceiling until the guard had gone back to his chair.

In between checks, he worked at the lashings on his wrists, which were nylon cord and therefore dead easy to untie with his teeth. When his hands were finally free, he simply lay on the bunk and listened and thought. He was in no hurry. It was still far too early.

He had no watch, but he had an excellent mental clock, developed long ago in other cells. The sounds of the change of guards outside came just about when he expected it. The relief guard seemed less nervous. The eyes that occasionally looked in through the inspection slot were blue. Still Hovik did nothing.

Finally, a couple of hours or so after the guard change, Hovik heard the footsteps of another man and a muffled clatter as the guard sprang to his feet. The officer or NCO said something unintelligible; the guard replied. The slot snapped open and this time a second pair of eyes studied the interior of the cell for a minute or so.

When the inspecting visitor had gone, Hovik sat on the edge of the bunk and, moving very quickly, began taking off his clothes. He got out of the camouflaged bush jacket, kicked off his boots—they had not remembered to take the laces, but he had already untied and loosened them—and pulled off his threadbare jeans. Taking the single gray wool blanket from the bunk, he began to tear it quietly into several large pieces.

The blanket was barely sufficient to stuff the buttoned-up bush jacket and the waist section of the jeans, with just enough left to form a loosely wrapped bundle about the size of a football. Even then he had to remove his tee-shirt, socks, and headband to add to the stuffing. Tying the pants and jacket sections together with a bootlace, fixing the "head" in place with the other, he decided that this was about as unconvincing a dummy as he had ever seen. On the other hand, it ought to be good enough for this.

He stood on the edge of the bunk and found he could barely reach the light grill with his fingertips. Teetering unsteadily in bare feet, he almost fell before finally getting the end of the nylon cord through the grill and knotting it.

He hoisted the clothing dummy in one arm and wrapped the nylon cord about the bush jacket's collar, tying it in back with an ordinary knot—he had thought of making a regular noose, but decided that was unnecessary trouble—and stood back. From inside the cell the effect was ridiculous, the empty sleeves and pant legs dangling limply with nothing at the cuffs; but from outside, he hoped, the guard would see mainly the outline of the hanging figure, and would not in any case be likely to take the time for a really good look. And the loose, limber-necked head section did droop to one side in a convincing way.

Hovik stood on the bunk, back against the wall, next to

the door, and waited. He had to wait quite awhile, but that was all right. Waiting was something he was very good at.

At last there came the scrape of chair legs on the stone floor, the clack of a rifle being picked up by its sling, and the movement of boots. He heard Mackenzie's viewport open and close and then the steps of the guard outside his own cell.

The panel slid back. There was a half-second's silence and then, very softly but distinctly, Hovik heard the guard say, "Oh, Jesus *Christ*—"

The heavy door bolt rattled and clanked back. The door swung open and the guard took two steps forward, his eyes fixed in horror on the hanging dummy.

Hovik landed on him and slammed him hard against the stone wall, wrenching the rifle free with one hand, covering the opening mouth with the other. Lips flattened and teeth worked desperately against Hovik's palm for a moment as he bore the thrashing guard to the floor. The big muscles of Hovik's bare shoulders and back jumped into deep relief as he gave a violent wrenching heave.

There was a faint but audible cracking sound, like someone cracking a walnut. The guard gave one convulsive jerk and went completely limp. When Hovik released his hold the guard's head flopped loosely at an unnatural angle.

Hovik stood up, raising the guard's rifle. Still nearly naked, he padded to the cell door and checked the outer room, but there was no one in sight.

Quickly he moved to the door of Mackenzie's cell and threw the bolt and yanked the door open. Mackenzie stood staring at him. "Get out here," Hovik said urgently, but Mackenzie was already in motion.

Hovik handed over the guard's M16—Mackenzie's hands, he saw with satisfaction, were already free—and said, "Watch the hallway."

Stepping over the dead man on the floor, he untied the hanging dummy, and began retrieving his clothes. Relacing his boots cost more time than he liked, but there was no choice; he might need to be very fast and sure on his feet in the next few hours. He took the guard's cap, which had fallen off in the struggle, and pulled it on, stuffing his long black hair up out of sight. The guard was a smaller man than Hovik and the fatigue cap sat well back on Hovik's head; the effect was not very good, but at least it was a little less conspicuous. He turned the collar of his bush jacket up in back and decided there was nothing more he could do. Just have to keep his head down and avoid the bright lights—of course, he thought, that was the plan that had landed him here to begin with. He closed the cell door on the dead guard, took the rifle back from Mackenzie, and led the way out into the corridor.

The passageway was empty and the other rooms along it were dark. Hovik and Mackenzie walked rapidly and quietly, staying close to the wall, not speaking. It was only a little way to the junction with the main tunnel.

They were, by Hovik's best estimate, about a mile back into the mountain. He did not allow himself to think much about that.

The big main tunnel was nowhere near as busy as it had been earlier that night. Here and there troopers walked along singly or in informal groups, and there were guards at some of the side passages; a squad of men marched past in file, headed somewhere deeper inside the mountain, while Hovik and Mackenzie slouched along on the far side of the tunnel, heads down and faces averted. Most of the work details seemed to have stopped for the night.

They had gone perhaps a quarter of a mile when a voice from one of the side passages said sharply, "Hey! Hey, you two guys."

Hovik turned very fast, his thumb finding the M16's safety. But there was only a single trooper standing in the shadows, holding out a pack of cigarettes. An unlit cigarette dangled awkwardly from his lips.

He said, "Hey, either of you guys got any of them funny little matches, gimme a light for this thing?"

Mackenzie said, "Sure. Just a minute," and pretended to take something from his pocket. Stepping into the side tunnel, he held out his hand, palm down. "Here you go."

The trooper reached out, mumbling an indistinct thanks. Mackenzie's hand clamped around his outstretched wrist and pulled. The startled man opened his mouth, losing his cigarette, as he was yanked half around, and then his face went slack as Hovik smashed the butt of the M16 into the back of his head.

Hovik took the pack of cigarettes from the limp fingers and dropped it thoughtfully into his own pocket.

Mackenzie was still holding the man up, about to lower him to the floor, when another voice said, "What's going on here, men?"

Hovik kept his face turned away. Mackenzie, his own face masked by the top of the trooper's head, said, "Man had an accident here, Lieutenant. Seems to have hit his head."

"Oh?" The voice sounded tired. "Well, better get him to the train, get our alleged doctor to look at him, if the son of a bitch hasn't found some booze around this place and floated away again . . . go on, get a move on."

Mackenzie said, "Yes, sir." Together they maneuvered the unconscious man—dead, Hovik was pretty sure, but he hoped that didn't show—into position between them, his limp arms over their shoulders, his feet dragging the floor. As they moved away the voice behind them said, "Get down to supply tomorrow and find a hat that fits you, soldier. That thing looks like hell."

It was, Hovik realized instantly, the perfect cover. Carrying the limp body between them, bowed and stopped with obvious effort—actually the trooper wasn't all that heavy, but it looked good and gave them an excuse to keep their faces down—they walked openly up the tunnel, unchallenged and unquestioned, just a couple of soldiers helping their injured buddy. (God help our asses, Hovik thought, if some brilliant bastard thinks to go get a stretcher.) As they passed one group of troopers a man called out something, but Mackenzie merely made an impatient no-time-to-talk-now motion with one hand and they walked on.

The man between them was definitely not breathing. His boot toes made a soft dragging sound on the stone floor.

As they neared the tunnel entrance they began to encounter more people. The slave laborers were still at work clearing away the rubble that had camouflaged the tunnel entrance, guarded by weary-looking troopers. The forklift rolled past on its mysterious business. From somewhere nearby a string of loud curses suggested somebody's temper hadn't been improved by the late hours. Hovik guessed it was around two or three in the morning.

The guard at the tunnel entrance said, "The fuck happened here?"

"Hit his head," Mackenzie said without looking up. "Fell

over some stuff in the dark. Lieutenant Mitchell said take him to the train."

"Yeah?" The guard did not move out of their way. "You sure this ain't just a trick to get off night duty? I been hearing a lot of good stories, the last couple hours."

"Jesus," Mackenzie said, "you want to check with Mitchell, send somebody to get him. He'll be real happy about having to walk all the way up here just because you had a wild hair up your ass. Anyway," he added, "look at the blood on this poor bastard's head."

"Huh. Yeah, you're right. Sorry. Got my orders," the guard said, moving aside. "The Old Man put out the word to watch for anybody acting suspicious. Said they caught a couple of Communist spies awhile back, they might have some buddies sneaking around."

Then, as they walked past and started down the hillside: "Wait a minute. I better get some names here, just in case somebody asks."

Hovik said quietly, "Keep walking. Act like you don't hear him."

They were almost clear of the brightly lit area around the tunnel entrance. The guard yelled, "Hey, God damn it, I'm talking to you two. Name and unit. His too. Turn around and answer properly."

Still walking, Hovik called back, "Ah, quit bucking for a fucking stripe. We'll talk to you after we get this guy to the train."

"What?" The guard's voice was rising to a shout. "Don't gimme that shit! Who the hell are you, anyway? Halt," he screamed, "halt, you sonsabitches! You men there, somebody stop those—"

Dropping the dead trooper, Hovik whirled and took a single long step to one side, the M16 snapping into firing position in his hands. The guard was still getting his own rifle unslung when Hovik shot him through the chest, a quick three-round burst that knocked him back against the stone wall behind him. Before the body had hit the ground, Hovik and Mackenzie were running down the mountainside, taking great plunging strides, bootheels sliding in the loose scree. Off to the right a couple of men appeared in a patch of light, raising weapons, and Hovik snapped a fast burst in their direction to keep them out of it. Behind them a few shots were being fired, but nothing seemed to be coming very close.

They ran at an angle, across and down the mountainside, having no desire to get close to the train, where troopers were already starting to emerge from the darkened cars. Hovik thought of shooting out the nearest lights, but he would have had to stop and take careful aim and there was no time for that. Instead he fired a few unaimed shots at the largest group of troopers, just on general principles, and kept running.

It was a wild blind run down the steep rock-strewn slope, and Hovik fully expected to break a leg before they reached the bottom. But somehow they reached the darkness beyond the lighted work areas, bullets popping and snapping all around them now, and seconds later they were half-staggering across the railroad track a little way past the silent locomotives.

Mackenzie said, "Follow the track or make for the woods?" He didn't say it very clearly; he was fighting for air.

"Woods, I guess," Hovik said, not breathing all that easily himself. "No, wait, let's try something—"

He led the way along the weedy spur track, running fast

between the rails, the M16 at high port across his chest. Behind them, up on the mountainside and along the train, all hell was definitely breaking loose. People were firing weapons in what sounded like all possible directions and voices were shouting orders. Some damn fool was even blowing a whistle.

The point buggy was a big black shape in the darkness ahead. As they came close a man stood up and leaned over the sandbags. "The hell's going on back there?" he asked sleepily.

"Listen," Hovik said, stepping up to the side of the truck, and shot the man through the head. And wished instantly he'd gotten close and used his hands, but it was too late now; the shot had been heard and the racket behind them suddenly took a definite and alarming direction. Bullets began to come by in the dark, sounding entirely too close.

Mackenzie said, "Can you start this thing?"

"Probably," Hovik said, grabbing one of the welded-on handholds and swinging himself up. The doors of the cab had been welded shut so that crude slabs of boiler-iron armor could be bolted to the outside; it was necessary to climb over the sandbags and enter through the big torch-cut opening in the back of the cab. He ducked under the dash, feeling about, only to discover that the keys were still in place.

"Probably?" Mackenzie said behind him.

"No sweat," Hovik called back. "Drove one of these a long time ago. Come to think of it, I stole that one too. Hang on."

Mackenzie was already swinging the big fifty-caliber machine gun around on its pedestal mount, hauling back the arming handle with a loud metallic clang and letting it snap forward, doing it again to make sure. There was no real way to aim, though his eyes were getting used to the darkness now; but he pointed the huge machine gun in the general direction of the train, where rifles were flashing all along the track and the mountainside, and opened fire.

The sound of the fifty-caliber was enormous. A long snake's tongue of flame licked from the end of the long barrel and fat orange tracers arced through the night, sailing back toward the train and disappearing, here and there glancing off rocks and rails. Mackenzie raised the muzzle a little and saw his tracers striking amid the winking flashes of the rifles. He had no idea whether he was hitting anything, but if nothing else it felt a great deal better than simply getting shot at.

The engine began to growl and rumble, its sound nearly lost in the steady roar of the fifty-caliber. Hovik said, "All *right*," and reached for the gearshift.

The point buggy jerked into motion, taking Mackenzie by surprise; he staggered and fired several half-inch rounds at the sky before regaining his balance. The rifle flashes were getting much closer now, despite his efforts, and a few bullets were beginning to whang off the armor and thump into the sandbags. Clinging to the big gun for support, half-blinded by its muzzle flash, he felt the truck beginning to pick up speed.

There were, Hovik discovered, no headlights at all. He leaned out the window, trying to watch the track, but he could see nothing. "Mackenzie!" he yelled between bursts of the fifty-caliber. "God *damn*, Mackenzie—"

Mackenzie heard him, finally. "What?"

"Watch the fucking *track*." They had rounded the curve now, where the track followed the contour of the mountain, and were rolling rapidly across the open meadow. "Watch for the switch."

Mackenzie leaned out until he could see past the cab,

holding onto a grabiron and straining to see. The moon was down but the night was clear, and the stars gave enough light to pick up the silvery streaks of the rails. The sounds of gunfire had grown more distant, but the pursuit clearly had not been given up yet.

He saw the switch ahead, or rather he saw the curving forks of the Y where the starlight caught the rails. He banged on the cab with his fist and Hovik hit the brakes. There was a steel-on-steel screech from the wheels and the point buggy slid to a stop.

It had been too late; they had overrun the switch. Hovik cursed, yanked at the gearshift, and backed up. "You know how to throw a switch?" he yelled at Mackenzie.

"No. Tell me what to—"

"Never mind." Hovik scrambled back through the hole in the cab, vaulted over the sandbags, dropped to the ground, and grabbed the rusty lever. There was a grinding squeal and the points moved reluctantly over and into place. Hovik clambered back aboard, shifted into gear, and drove slowly through the switch and along the left-curving arm of the Y. The shots from back up the track were getting closer again. Something whined off the iron armor next to his elbow.

When the second switch appeared Mackenzie said, "I'll get this one," and dropped to the ground before Hovik had the point buggy completely stopped.

But it wasn't as easy as it had looked when Hovik did it. Mackenzie hauled at the iron bar with all his strength but nothing moved. Bullets were starting to come over again. He yelled, "Hovik!"

Hovik was already on the way. Together they bent and heaved, grunting in unison, boots digging into the loose gravel. There was a sudden loud creak and the points began to move. Still it took both of them to throw the switch all the way.

"They didn't use that one when they came in," Hovik said as they scuttled back onto the point buggy. "Rusty son of a bitch probably ain't been moved in ten, fifteen years. Wonder we could move it at all—"

He shifted and let in the clutch. The point buggy rumbled through the switch and onto the heavier rails of the branch line. They began to roll down the long grade, across the mountain meadow and toward the tree line. Hovik accelerated and shifted. "All *right*," he said happily. "Now we get our asses out of here in style."

It was a strange sensation to be operating a truck that steered itself. He leaned back, holding his hands above the locked steering wheel. "Look, Mac, no hands. We can drive all the way home," he said. "Nearly, anyway. No need to stop and jack around with that old truck we left in the woods. Got us a fifty into the deal, too. Man, I'm gonna figure some way to stash this thing till all this is over—we can use it to go some places."

Mackenzie was standing up again, looking back the way they had come, across the meadow toward the dark bulk of the mountain. He could still see the glow of the lights but the shooting seemed to have stopped. He said, "You don't suppose they'll want us badly enough to uncouple one of those locomotives and come after us?"

"Forget it," Hovik said, slowing for the first curve. "You got no idea the time it takes to start one of those big bastards up cold, get it rolling—the start we got, they'd never catch us. Besides, Decker ain't going to risk wrecking one of his engines in a chase in the dark, just because we pissed him off."

They were moving fast now, the old motor bellowing and blaring, the wheels clacking noisily over the rail joints. Great dark masses of trees slipped past on either side. Overhead the stars looked as big as baseballs in the clear black mountain sky.

Hovik said, "Yeah, we'll be home before you know it—"

The engine coughed and missed. Hovik pumped the pedal, declutched, shifted down. The engine missed again and then died.

"*Oh*, shit." Hovik shifted quickly into neutral. "I knew it was going too good. Sonsabitches ran this thing damn near dry and didn't fill up again. Probably figured there was plenty of time to refuel before they had to go anywhere."

"We're out of gas?" Mackenzie said. "Or diesel fuel, rather?"

"Seems like. God damn it." Hovik pounded the locked steering wheel with his fist. "Oh well, we may not be fucked yet. Wait a minute before we get out and start walking. I think just maybe . . ."

The point buggy continued to roll. It was not moving as fast as it had under power, but it was moving steadily and it did not seem to be losing any more speed. "Good," Hovik said. "We got just enough of a downhill grade to keep rolling. All the way to the main line, if I remember right."

It was an eerie sensation, rolling briskly along without any sound except the squeal and clack of the wheels on the rails. Hovik dug out the pack of cigarettes. "Wonder if any of the guys on this thing had a light." He felt and fumbled around on top of the dash. "Ah. Here we go."

He stuck a cigarette between his lips and struck a paper match. The sudden flare of light illuminated his lined face and bristling beard for a moment as he dragged on the cigarette. "Damn, been a hell of a long time since I had any of these. Joe Jack mixes up some shit from dried willow bark and leaves and all, smokes it in this pipe he made, and some of the young guys do the same, but I never could stand it myself." He blew out smoke with a grateful sigh. "I quit a lot of years ago, and I guess I'll quit again when this pack's empty, but man, right now this is what I needed."

He held out the pack to Mackenzie. "Want one?"

Mackenzie shook his head. "Never acquired the habit. Thanks."

"Hazardous to your health, huh?" Hovik stuffed the pack back in his bush jacket pocket and grinned. "Sure was hazardous to that poor bastard's health, wasn't it? Jesus Christ, I busted jail a few times in my life, but that's got to be the weirdest number ever."

He laughed suddenly. "I just realized something. That son of a bitch Decker got my forty-five, you know? Really pisses me off, I had that piece a long time, but I got it in another break to begin with. Took it off a guard," he said. "So I guess it goes around and it comes around, huh?"

They rolled along for mile after mile, propelled only by gravity. Now and then they slowed down on a flatter stretch, but their momentum carried them on and the long steady downgrades gave them so much speed sometimes Hovik had to use the brakes on curves. "Sandbags and armor," Hovik said, "all that weight's really helping pull us down this mountain."

But not long afterward Hovik began to apply the brakes cautiously, peering intently ahead at the faint twin lines of the track. "I think we're about getting to where we left the truck," he said. "Watch for where the road crosses the track. As I remember, that was the last—yeah. Here."

He stopped the point buggy just past the dirt road and set the brake. "Oh, man, we better hope we can get that cranky old mother started," he said as they climbed out of the cab. "I don't know, but I'm not sure we can get this armored doodlebug rolling again from a dead stop. Not that much grade hereabouts and we sure as hell ain't tough enough to push it."

As they walked up the dirt road Mackenzie said, "Why not just stick with what we had? We seemed to be doing all right."

"Yeah, but once we hit the main line it's all level, even climbs a little bit before it starts to drop down toward that bridge. And then we'd have a hell of a long walk to get home. Call me lazy, but I'd rather not just now."

The old truck was still sitting under the trees. They pushed it toward the road, with a good deal of grunting and cursing, and aimed it down the short slope. "Know soon enough," Hovik said, and slid behind the wheel.

For a minute or so it seemed as if they were in for an even longer walk, as the engine burped and wheezed and the transmission whined and Hovik fought the worn-out clutch. But then, just as they were almost out of momentum, a couple of cylinders began to fire, and then a couple more, and by the time they crossed the track the engine was clattering raggedly and making noisy pops from the exhaust.

Hovik let it warm up for a few minutes and then started slowly down the dirt road. Only one of the headlights was working and that only on low beam; he took it slowly and kept the gears low.

"Let's go home," he said to Mackenzie. "Judith's gonna kick my ass, she finds out how we spent the night."

13

Mackenzie said, "Decker's got to be stopped."

"Sounds like it," Joe Jack Mad Bull agreed. "But how?"

Judith said, "Find a way. Mackenzie's right. He's got to be stopped before he turns what's left of the country into a slaughterhouse." She closed her eyes and shuddered visibly. "An *atomic* slaughterhouse, for God's sake, I can't get over that. After all that's happened, that there's anyone crazy enough to . . . no, you've got to find some way to stop him."

Hovik said suddenly, flatly, "No."

They were sitting around the long table in Hovik's cabin. It was a little after daybreak. No one had had much sleep.

Now three pairs of slightly red-rimmed eyes were staring at Hovik, who said again, "No. Nobody's going to stop Decker, nobody's going to try."

His palms were flat on the tabletop in front of him. He looked straight ahead, as if seeing something beyond the opposite wall. The scar on his forehead stood out against the suddenly tightened skin of his face.

Joe Jack said, "Hey, Hovik, all right, it's hard to see how we can do it, but we oughta at least talk about—"

"I don't want Decker stopped," Hovik said, ignoring him. "I'll do whatever I have to do to keep anybody else from stopping him."

Judith's mouth opened. Nothing came out.

"What's got to happen," Hovik went on, "we got to find some way to *destroy* the son of a bitch, *and* his whole setup, all that heavy shit he's taking out of that mountain. And if we can't destroy him, then by God we leave him the hell alone and let him get out of here."

Mackenzie said suddenly, "I see what you're saying."

"Yeah, you should. You saw the same stuff I saw." Hovik looked at the others for the first time. "Stop him? Hell, we could do that easy enough. Wouldn't be any big trick to derail that train—I'm surprised nobody's done it already. Or we could get some of that dynamite Billy found and take out the lead engine. Lots of ways to make sure he doesn't get that train out of these mountains."

Mackenzie nodded. "And then he's stuck here with his Army and his missiles and his bombs, so he starts his war right here. You're right. That's even worse than letting him go."

Judith sighed. "Philosophically speaking, I suppose that's the wrong attitude. I mean, you could argue that it's better for Decker to be rampaging around a thinly populated area like this than to have him going after the cities—greater good of the greater number, and all that. But I'm not a philosopher, I'm a mother. And I live here myself."

Joe Jack said, "Hey, are we all listening to ourselves? Let's think about this a minute." He began doodling on the tabletop with his finger. "We got this General with an army—all right, he ain't a real General and his Army ain't much of an army, but they sure as hell add up to a lot more than we got here. They got armor, artillery, everything but aviation, and on top of that the bastards got *nukes* now . . . and we're sitting here, we can put, what, maybe twenty rifles on the line tops, and we're talking about how we got to whack this guy and his Army out. Like that was something we could decide to do if we happened to feel like it." He shook his head. "I mean, I'm all for it in principle, but damn if I see how."

Judith said, "Didn't you tell me once how Geronimo took on the whole U.S. Army with about twenty men?"

"Yeah, but look who finally won," Joe Jack said gloomily. "And Geronimo wasn't up against nukes."

Hovik said, "Only one possible way to do it, that I can see."

Mackenzie looked at him. "The bridge?"

"The bridge." Hovik stood up. "Come on, let's go have a look at it. Go get Billy Blackhorse," he said to Joe Jack. "Something this crazy, we could use some input from an authentic weirdo. Anyway, he's the one knows where the dynamite is."

He rubbed his eyes. "Christ, I wish we'd ripped off some of that coffee. . . ."

They stood between the rails at the center of the high bridge and looked down at the massive structure of steel and concrete. Mackenzie said, "Forget it."

"You can tell that easy?" Joe Jack said. "I mean, we don't even know yet how much dynamite we've got—"

"It doesn't matter. Look at this thing." Mackenzie kicked

dispiritedly at a rail. "In the movies they were always blowing up bridges and it looked so simple—they'd just tie a bundle of dynamite to any old beam or girder and wham bam, great special effects, down goes the bridge with all the bad guys. And you might do it, too," he said, "if you were talking about a little old wooden trestle or an old-fashioned single-span iron truss. But this is a modern steel-and-concrete railroad bridge, for God's sake."

Hovik looked down between the crossties at the river far below. "All I know about dynamite, stuff like that," he said, "I had a little demo training in the Corps, then I shared a cell for awhile with an old safe man. You're the guy had all those engineering courses at whatever college it was. You're saying you can't blow this thing?"

"With enough time, enough manpower, enough explosive, sure." Mackenzie kicked the rail again, looking angry at it. "I could dump this thing into the gorge in as many pieces as you wanted. But you're asking a lot more, Hovik. You said it yourself: we can't just stop that train."

"Right," Hovik nodded. "Got to blow the bridge with the train *on* it. Last thing we need is to strand the bastards in our back yard."

"Exactly. And that would involve a precise and massive demolition setup, and I doubt seriously if we've got that much dynamite available—leaving aside, of course, the very strong likelihood of blowing ourselves up the first time we touch that unstable old stuff—and I know damn well *I* don't have the technical knowledge to do it. This is a job for a top-level demolitions expert, and he'd probably laugh in our faces at that."

"Shit," Joe Jack said. "We need one of those small nukes Decker talked about."

"I hate to admit it," Mackenzie nodded, "but that's about what we'd need to be sure of blowing this span. I'm telling you, a modern bridge is one hell of a tough structure."

Billy Blackhorse looked up from where he squatted between the rails. He had been studying the bridge with profound interest. "I read in a book," he said, "the Allies captured this bridge across the Rhine in 1945 and the Germans tried again and again to blow it up, and they never succeeded."

"Okay, okay," Joe Jack said. "I believe you about taking out the whole bridge. But why can't we just put some charges right under the track and blow the damn train off the bridge? Don't tell me you can't do that either."

"Hell, anybody could do it that way," Hovik said. "In fact you could probably derail the train on the bridge without even using explosives—sabotage the track or something. Only Decker's not stupid. He'll have his people check out that bridge like Feds looking for prints, man, and they'll find anything we put anywhere near this track. Look how this thing's built," Hovik pointed out. "All open girders and the wind blowing through. We'd never hide the charges where they wouldn't spot them."

"Not big enough charges to do the job, anyway," Mackenzie agreed. "To say nothing of fuse wire and Primacord and so on. They'll recover the point buggy when they get to where we left it, if not sooner, and even without it they'd just check the bridge out on foot."

"Son of a bitch." Joe Jack started to kick at the rail, too, but then he remembered he was wearing moccasins.

"That's another thing," Mackenzie added. "Even if we had enough dynamite to take out the whole span, and the expertise to use it, it wouldn't be easy hiding that kind of setup."

"So what the hell do we do?" Joe Jack said disgustedly. "Sit up on the cliffs and throw rocks at them?"

Mackenzie said, "Well—"

He stopped, staring out across the gorge at empty space, seeing in his mind a sudden clear picture of a pair of small grubby hands smashing a rock into a tin-can locomotive.

Billy Blackhorse said, "I guess we—"

"Shut up," Mackenzie said in a strange voice. Everyone stared at him.

"Everybody be quiet a minute," he added. He was looking up at the cliffs now, studying the eroded knobs and crags along the rim of the gorge. "Hovik," he said, "do you still have those binoculars?"

Hovik shook his head. "You know they took them last night."

Billy Blackhorse said, "Here, use mine. They're not very good," he apologized. "I dropped them in the creek last—"

Mackenzie waved him into silence. The others watched while Mackenzie studied something up near the top of the cliffs.

Finally Mackenzie lowered the binoculars. There was a peculiar look on his face. "Billy," he said, "let's see that dynamite of yours."

As they walked back along the bridge Hovik said, "Come on, Mackenzie. What's happening?"

"I'm not sure yet," Mackenzie said, still in that faraway voice. "But I think we just may have a way to bust Decker's choo-choo. . . ."

A couple of hours later, standing at the entrance of the derelict mine, Mackenzie said, "Billy, when they told me you were crazy I thought they were being too harsh. Now—"

He looked at Billy Blackhorse with what was almost awe. "You went in there by yourself? And nobody knew you were here?"

"Pawnees," Joe Jack said, as if that explained everything. "Hovik, you got that old carbide lamp working yet?"

From the other side of the parked pickup truck Hovik growled something indistinct.

"Finally found a use for that thing," Joe Jack remarked. "I was gonna use it for jacklighting deer, only we never really needed to—hey," he said to Billy Blackhorse, "how the hell did *you* see anything in there?"

"I made a torch," Billy said. "It wasn't very big, but I could see well enough for what I was doing."

"He made a torch." Joe Jack closed his eyes. "Ten-year-old dynamite, blasting caps and Primacord all over the place, and he walked in there waving a God-damned torch. You're a terrible person, Billy. You're trying to make me crazy."

"I'm not all that wild about the carbide lamp," Mackenzie said. "In fact we're all insane to be going anywhere near that dynamite. You do understand what happens to dynamite with the passage of time? Among other things, it sweats. It's basically nothing but nitroglycerine mixed with an inert base so it can be handled and controlled. When it sits around long enough, especially if the temperature gets too high, the nitro sweats and pools and crystallizes and various other fun things."

"Yeah," Hovik said, coming around the truck with the carbide lantern hissing in his hand. "Then, you look hard at it with more than one eyeball at a time, it rains fool all week. That's what the old safe guy told me, anyway."

He started toward the mine entrance. "You guys coming or not?"

* * *

The dynamite was stored a short way down the entrance tunnel. A section of a side passage had been fenced off with floor-to-ceiling sections of heavy steel mesh, framed with thick timbers. There was a door that had been locked, but the padlock lay broken on the dusty floor. Mackenzie looked at Billy Blackhorse. "You broke the lock?"

Billy nodded. "See, there's lots of tools down here, I found this big old hammer and—"

"Stop." Joe Jack went over and banged his head softly against the rock wall. "Don't tell me any more," he said in a hollow voice. "I don't want to know about it."

Hovik said, "Christ, there's a lot of it. How many cases you figure that is?"

"Hard to tell," Mackenzie said, "the way they've got it stacked. Enough for what I've got in mind, if it can be done at all."

He moved cautiously forward, stepping into the cage, trying to read the markings on the wax-coated cases. "Aim that light a little higher, Hovik . . . Du Pont Extra, that's pretty good as I remember."

"Good high nitro content," Hovik said. "More bang, but more chance of it going crazy in ten years, too. For Christ's sake be careful in there."

Mackenzie saw that the nearest box had been opened. Billy's work, no doubt, and he decided against asking the details. Joe Jack was right; it was better not to know, at least while they were down here looking at it. He reached out and ran a finger very gently over the surfaces of the top layer of sticks.

"Doesn't seem to have exuded any," he said in a low voice. There was no logical reason to speak in subdued tones;

it was just something they were all doing instinctively. "Of course it's nice and cool down here, probably stays a fairly constant temperature."

"Summer's not very hot up here anyway," Hovik offered. "If that helps."

"Right . . . I don't know, it may be okay. Just have to handle it exactly as we'd handle pure nitro."

"I don't know how to tell you this," Joe Jack said, "but as a general thing I don't handle nitro at *all*. Pure or dirty."

Mackenzie stepped away from the dynamite and considered the other supplies at hand. Plenty of caps, lots of detonating cord—that was good, they'd need it, have to test a few samples to make sure—some remote-control gear that was almost certainly useless now, and, sitting in one corner, a big box that proved to contain an old-fashioned hand-push generator. There were also several large coils of wire. "All we need," he said to the others, "assuming it all works."

"You want to start moving it out now?" Hovik asked.

"Not yet. No point in taking that kind of risk until I'm sure we can bring this off." He walked back out of the cage and turned toward the distant rectangle of sunlight. "Come on, let's go back to the bridge area. How hard is it to get at that rimrock, up at the top of the cliff on the east side of the gorge?"

"No problem," Hovik said, sounding puzzled. "Dirt road goes right up there, it's open and flat on top. Mind telling me what you're working on?"

"Soon as I've checked something out. Billy, you said there were tools and things down here? Did you happen to find any good stout nylon rope?"

* * *

Joe Jack Mad Bull, clinging to a half-grown juniper with white-knuckled fingers, leaned out over the eroded lip of the cliff top and said, "All right, just a little bit lower."

Behind him Hovik, heels dug into rainpockets in the rock, let out another foot of the yellow rope that ran through his hands, wrapped itself once around the wind-twisted pine tree, and stretched guitar-string taut to disappear over the edge of the cliff.

Twenty feet below, Mackenzie dangled in space at the end of the rope and studied the pattern of cracks and crevices that seamed the cliff face before him. A rusty singlejack hammer, taken from the mine, dangled from his right hand. Now and then he chipped experimentally at spots on the rock wall, or broke fragments from protruding knobs and corners and examined them before tossing them over his shoulder into the enormous emptiness behind and beneath him.

Under his swinging feet there was a great deal of open space, but that did not bother him. He had hung above much, much greater spaces in his day.

He looked down, now, twisting about like a spider at the end of his line, and surveyed the gorge and the bridge. It was not a straight-down view; directly below him, halfway down the cliffside, a big rock shoulder protruded sharply out above the gorge. Below that the cliff turned gradually into an extremely steep slope, rather than a true vertical precipice, and at the level of the bridge a surefooted man might even have been able to stand upright on the scree-covered surface. Not far below bridge level, where the river had encountered an older, harder layer of rock, the cliffs again fell sheer and unbroken to the river's banks.

The bridge itself did not cut directly across the river at right angles. Rather it spanned the lower gorge at an angle of forty-five degrees or so, crossing in the middle of a horseshoe bend, the tracks running along a kind of great blasted-out shelf in the rock for a quarter-mile or so below the bridge, before turning through a deep cut into the valley beyond.

From where he hung, the bridge looked very small. It was not entirely an illusion, he realized; the railroad bridge *was* a narrow target, much narrower than the nearby highway span. And the variables and imponderables were so numerous as to outweigh the givens. Still, it was a better chance than anything else they had come up with.

He looked up at Joe Jack's anxious face, hovering twenty feet above, and jerked his thumb upward. "Okay," he yelled. "Bring me up."

Back up on the rimrock he said to Hovik, "How long do you figure we have?"

"Hm. Well, figuring all the work they got to do, humping all that big stuff down the mountain and loading it onto the train, mostly by hand too—and like Decker said, you don't just kick a missile down the hillside or toss a nuke into the nearest boxcar—hell, I don't know, let's see. Figure they'll work at night some, but not the really tricky stuff. . . ."

He scratched his head. "Best I make it, it's got to take them today and tomorrow, minimum. Maybe part of another day, but I wouldn't count on it. Say they pull out day after tomorrow, early in the morning. That long enough for what you had in mind?"

"I think so. If we don't lose too much time moving that dynamite."

"Hell, that won't take too long. I'll take charge of that end of it." Hovik hesitated. "Look, I could send Joe Jack and a couple of guys to buy us some more time. Tear up the track, maybe snipe at the work crews a little—"

"No, I don't think so. We need all the available workers here anyway." Mackenzie looked at Billy Blackhorse. "How's your math, Billy?"

"Top of my class in school," Billy said proudly. "Made the finals in the Oklahoma state competition, before we had to move to LA—"

"He's good," Joe Jack told Mackenzie. "Sits around during his spare time with these old math books, working problems just for laughs."

"Great, you can help me figure this out." Mackenzie sighed. "Christ, what I'd give for a computer right now."

Billy said, "What about a slide rule?"

Mackenzie blinked at him. "You've got a slide rule?"

"Sure. Found it in this old school building, taught myself to use it with this book. Simple principle when you think about it."

"Well, I'll be damned. Sure, get it, it'll save a lot of time. Also we need some paper and pencils—"

"Excuse me," Hovik said patiently, "but before you two big brains get all hung up in your calculations, how about letting us ordinary grunts in on the big secret plan?"

"What? Oh, sorry," Mackenzie said. "Well, look, the basic idea's pretty simple. You see that rock formation there . . . ?"

Judith said, "That's crazy. Will it work?"

"Damn if I know," Hovik said sleepily in the darkness of

the bedroom. "Mackenzie seems to know what he's doing, that's encouraging. On the other hand he's got Billy helping him. All I know, it's the only shot we got."

Alice Santana said, "Mac, we need to talk." But Mackenzie was already asleep.

14

Standing on the rimrock, his back to the still-shadowy gorge, Joe Jack Mad Bull said, "All right, boys and girls, everybody pay attention. I'm going to say this crap one God-damned time."

Lined up in front of him, shuffling their feet and looking around a little nervously, his crew tried to pay attention. Behind them the eastern sky was showing a pale yellow streak all along the horizon. Better make this quick, he thought, or I'll have the rising sun in my eyes.

He looked at them a moment, all the same, before going on. Almost the whole adult and adolescent population of the camp was there; he realized suddenly that he had never before seen them all lined up at once. He would have given a good deal just then for a camera and film.

"You all know about this bunch of paramils with the train," he said. "Most of you already heard stories about how bad they are. Believe me, it's worse than you heard. Soon as there's time, we'll tell you the whole story. Right now, all that matters is we're gonna take them out.

"You see over there, where I'm pointing," he said over

a low murmur among the ranks, "see that big knob of rock that juts out from the cliff, the one that looks sort of like a great big fist?" It didn't, really; Joe Jack just thought that sounded good. "Okay, Mac and Billy got it figured out how we can bust that whole thing loose and it'll sail down off the cliff and smash the shit out of the train and probably the bridge too. It's got to be timed just right, but that's Mac's department. What we've got to do today is get it set up. We got some dynamite on the way," he added as several hands began waving. "But we can't just set it off any old place. Got to be placed just so, and that's gonna mean making some holes in the rock, making some cracks bigger, blistering some hands."

Somebody in the back said, "That thing? Jesus, it's the size of a house."

"Well, not *that* big. Maybe a small house trailer, though," Joe Jack said. "Anyway, you can see what a hell of an impact there's gonna be if it hits just right. If it doesn't, it's just gonna scare the shit out of a lot of fish. So everybody do what you're told and don't jack around."

He pointed again, this time to the ropes that ran over the edge of the cliff, their upper ends tied to trees. "Mac and Billy are down there right now, hanging their asses out in the breeze, fixing up a bunch of lines and loops and spikes and so on, so we can work on the cliff face. Don't worry, only a few people will be doing that, we've got plenty to do up here too. Anybody's scared of heights, for Christ's sake say so because later on we're gonna be handling dynamite and we don't need nobody to be nervous."

He gave them an evil grin. "And then if there's anybody just generally scared of *work*, well, that's okay, they can go back to camp and help Minnie and Frances take care of the kids."

One of the women groaned. "Oh, Jesus, those little bastards? Bring on the dynamite, I'm ready."

Joe Jack nodded. "Good enough. Nice to see democracy in action. All right, if you'll all follow me—"

At about the same time, down near the mine entrance, Hovik finished lashing down his load. Stepping back, surveying the boxes of dynamite and the old truck and the rutted road, he said aloud, "Well, if this don't take first prize."

The bed of the pickup had been padded with a couple of old mattresses, and the spaces between the dynamite boxes were filled with all the cushions and pillows he had been able to scrounge around camp. A network of ropes and rubber shock cords crisscrossed the truck bed, securing the boxes solidly in place. Dynamite, normally, was supposed to be unaffected by any reasonable amount of vibration and shock, but this batch was going through some kind of chemical change of life and God knew what might set it off. He figured it was even money the whole load would blow as soon as he started the engine.

He had been there since before dawn, working slowly and carefully, alone. He might have done the job faster with help, but he had decided there was no use risking anybody else's life when he could handle it by himself. Besides, if he got blown to bits by a stupid mistake or a clumsy move, he preferred it to be his own rather than someone else's.

Climbing into the cab, wishing very badly that he dared light one of his remaining cigarettes, he said to the truck, "Talk to Frank," and hit the starter.

***

Down on the cliff face, suspended in a rope sling, Mackenzie stuck a steel bar into the crack in the rock in front of him and wiggled it from side to side, probing. "Here," he said, withdrawing the bar.

Beside him, likewise suspended over emptiness, Billy Blackhorse took a thick charred stick and marked the rock with a circle where Mackenzie had stuck the bar. Mackenzie consulted a sheet of paper that he took from his pocket and said, "Four sticks there," and Billy nodded and made four marks in a row above the circle.

Mackenzie put the paper back in his pocket, very carefully, and tilted his head back to look up at the great dark overhang of the rock outcrop. There were a few spots that were going to be tricky and dangerous to get at. With technical rock-climbing gear the job would have been dead easy, but they were having to improvise.

"If we were doing this right," he said to Billy, "we'd do a series of shots instead of one big blast. Use small charges to enlarge some of these cracks and faults, gradually weaken the structure of the rock until that knob's just barely attached to the cliff, then at the key moment break it loose with a controlled blast . . . but we don't have good enough explosives to make that kind of calculations, even if we had the skills."

Billy gave him a buck-toothed grin. "Hey," he said, "you really were an astronaut, weren't you?"

Mackenzie sighed. "Yes."

"Ross Mackenzie. You were on the very last Moon shot. I went through all my stacks of old magazines last night, looking. I was just a kid when it happened," Billy said. "Boy, I used to know the names of all the astronauts, though, their ages, where they were from, everything. Like some kids with ball players or rock musicians."

He braced the soles of his tennis shoes against the rock and wrapped his hands around the rope. "You know something," he said as he and Mackenzie walked their way laterally across the cliff face to the next spot, "I had this idea when I was a kid, I wanted to be the first Indian astronaut." He laughed as Mackenzie stared at him. "Yeah, I know, crazy. My grandfather said, 'Forget it, boy, don't you go to that Moon. It'll just give the white people the idea to send us all up there.' "

He watched as Mackenzie hammered experimentally at the rock. "I finally figured it out," he said. "That's why you don't know much about demolitions but you know just about everything there is about ballistic curves and trajectories."

He said, "I know I'm talking too much, but can I ask just two more questions?"

Mackenzie lowered his hammer and nodded. "Sure."

"One: do we really, *really* know what we're doing?"

Mackenzie looked straight at him. "No."

Billy nodded thoughtfully. "Hm. Well, two: is this going to work?"

"Probably not," Mackenzie said.

"That's what I thought."

They grinned at each other suddenly. Mackenzie said, "Hand me that chisel."

"The loadspace situation," General Decker said to his officers, "has become critical. We are faced with an embarrassment of riches, gentlemen. With all the empty cars we brought along—I will refrain from pointing out how some of you argued, when we set out, that we were taking too many—and with all the rearranging of supplies and doubling-up of the troops, we're still going to be short."

"Dump the tanks," Captain Grimshaw suggested. "They haven't been that useful, and we've got better weapons now. That would give us two more flatcars."

"Yes," Decker nodded judiciously, "yes, Captain, I was thinking of that myself. If necessary we'll do so, though it will be a terrible job unloading those two dinosaurs. Anyone else have any ideas?"

No one else did. Decker said, "Come now, let's see some imagination. Hasn't anyone thought of one obvious measure?" Their faces said that they hadn't. "The laborers, gentlemen," Decker said impatiently. "The work crews. They're taking up several valuable boxcars, more really than they ever needed—we've pampered them, you know, we could have gotten all of them into half as many cars all along. And now, once our work is done here, will we really need them all? We'll need a few for various work details on the way home, of course—though we shouldn't have to work on the track so much, going back—but I'm sure we can dispense with most of them without major hardship."

He gave the officers a tight little smile. "The men will grumble, of course, at losing the services of the females, but since they'll be on their way home, they won't grumble too much."

Grimshaw said, "How many do we drop, sir?"

Decker raised his eyebrows. "Does anyone seriously pretend we know, other than approximately, how many of these people we have at present? Has anyone been keeping track?" No one responded. Decker said, "It's simple enough, Captain. Move them all into some of the dormitory chambers in the mountain—easier to guard them there anyway, not that they're going to be doing much sleeping—and then, when we're ready to leave, pack as many as you can into one boxcar. That ought to be enough."

"And the others?"

"Well, what would you recommend? Abandon them to a slow end in this wilderness? Or, perhaps, to be subverted and organized by those two Bolshevik saboteurs we captured and lost," he glared at Lieutenant Mitchell, "the other night? For God's sake, Captain, don't be fatuous. Shoot them," he said, "take them around to the far side of the mountain in manageable groups and shoot them. What's so complicated about that?"

Hovik parked the truck half a mile back down the road and walked the rest of the way to the rimrock. As soon as he was clear of the truck he got out a cigarette and lit it, the first thing he had done in haste all morning. His hands were not shaking but they felt as if they should be.

Up on the rimrock he found a scene of impressive activity. People hurried here and there carrying tools and coils of rope; others hauled on ropes, swung hammers, rappeled almost casually over the cliff's edge. From various points came the ringing of hammers on steel and rock. A couple of the smaller women were walking about with buckets of water and gourd dippers.

Joe Jack was standing a little way from the edge of the cliff, driving a small wedge into the head end of a hammer handle to tighten it. "Damn tools we got out of that mine yesterday," he said to Hovik, "handles dried out and shrank, few even rotted. You get the stuff okay?"

"Down the hill. I got to go back a couple more times, though, I couldn't carry much with all that padding in there."

He looked around. "Jesus, you really got everybody busting ass, don't you? Where's Mackenzie?"

"Hanging on a rope somewhere down on the cliff, like a God-damned caterpillar. Where he's been all morning." Joe Jack laughed. "You know what the kids are starting to call him? Mad Mac."

"Billy's with him?"

"Yeah. You were right, Frank. That dude's got balls on his balls, funny face or not." Joe Jack looked around. "Want me to send some people down to unload the dynamite?"

"Nah, I might as well. Looks like everybody up here's got something to do." He spotted Judith sitting nonchalantly at the edge, tying the end of a rope to the bail of a bucket full of loose tools. Her feet dangled free over the void. "God *damn*, Joe Jack, everybody's getting a little too brave up here, you know? I mean, hell, we're gonna be handling dynamite this afternoon. Somebody forgets to be scared of that stuff, boom."

"I'll keep an eye on the cowboys and cowgirls." Joe Jack looked at Hovik. "Sure you don't want to trade jobs for awhile, let me go get the next load?"

"I'll take it. Rather be doing that than working up here." Hovik dropped his voice. "Tell you the truth, Joe Jack, heights always make me nervous as hell."

By midafternoon Hovik had brought up the last of the dynamite and the holes had been prepared more or less to Mackenzie's satisfaction. Now Mackenzie sent all but a few people back to camp; there was, he said, no point in endangering more people than necessary.

"Besides," he said to Hovik and Joe Jack, "the fewer

people getting in each other's way up here, the less chance of an accident."

Joe Jack was staring at the rock knob. "What I don't get," he said, "if that dynamite's as fucked-up as you say, how can you be sure how much to use? You know, to kick that thing out the way you want?"

"Oh, no, we're not trying to launch it from here like some kind of missile." Mackenzie pointed down into the gorge. "All we're going to do is break it loose from the cliff and let it tumble straight on down until it hits that protruding shoulder of rock. That ought to kick it out far enough to hit the bridge. I don't really expect to hit the train itself," he said. "But if we can register a hit almost anywhere on the bridge while the train's on it, that ought to be enough to cause a derailment, and then the train goes into the river."

Joe Jack scratched his head. "Why do I feel like Wiley Coyote? Go look at the label on that dynamite again, I bet it's from the Acme Company." To Hovik he said, "Well, at least you're done driving it around. I bet you just about got a puckered asshole by now."

Hovik shrugged. "Yeah, but nothing happened. Maybe we were worried about nothing."

"Maybe," Mackenzie mused. "After all, we were only assuming it had gone cranky. And normally, you know, dynamite's very stable and reasonably safe to handle—if it's still in its original condition, it shouldn't go off from vibration or shock. You could toss a fresh stick of dynamite off this cliff and nothing would happen."

Half an hour later, standing at the edge of the cliff, Larry Bushyhead started to hand a single stick of dynamite to Joe Jack. His hands were sweaty and his palms were blistered;

he had been working hard all day. Suddenly the stick of dynamite slipped from his hands and shot gracefully over the edge into space.

Larry Bushyhead said, "Oh, shit."

Everybody stood absolutely still.

A few seconds later—it seemed like a very *long* few seconds—a flat, muffled boom drifted up from the depths of the gorge.

Hovik looked at Mackenzie. "Stable, huh?"

When he had all the charges placed and capped and connected with Primacord, Mackenzie took one last look around and said, "I think that's it. Let's run those wires out."

Carrying the big spool of wire between them on a jack handle, Joe Jack and Larry Bushyhead walked behind Mackenzie to a point far back from the rimrock, between a couple of clumps of wind-deformed cedars. "Too bad," Mackenzie said, "our man on the blaster isn't going to be able to see the results of his work. But that rock all along the cliff is too unstable—I don't know how much of that rimrock may go, just from sympathetic vibration. I'd run this wire even farther back, only then there's no way for him to see the signal."

He looked at Billy Blackhorse. "It's your dynamite, Billy. You want to be the one to set it off?"

Billy's large Adam's apple went up and down several times. "Yeah," he got out finally, his voice a little higher than usual. "Yeah, if you want me to."

"Okay, let's move back down the road and have a little training session. . . ."

Down on the road, near the parked truck, Mackenzie showed Billy how the plunger generator worked. "What you've got to remember," he said, "you're trying to crank out enough electricity to fire electrical blasting caps. The same principle as kick-starting a motorcycle, you've done that? Okay, try it."

He hooked up an extra blasting cap to the blaster's terminals with lengths of wire and said, "Try now. No, you can't just push it down, you've got to *slam* it down. Put your weight on it all at once and try to knock the bottom out of the generator box."

Billy Blackhorse nodded and gave a mighty downwards shove. The blasting cap popped sharply, a little puff of smoke rising in a miniature eruption. Mackenzie said, "All right, you've got it. Let's go home. Take the box along, Billy, we'll bring it back in the morning."

To the two young men who stood beside the truck, Hovik said, "We'll have some relief guards out to spell you around midnight. Don't get trigger-happy when they show up. And don't go grabassing around by that cliff in the dark."

The sun was starting to go down.

Stretching out across the bed, watching Judith brush her hair, Hovik said, "I'm getting too old for this life, you know that?"

"The hell you are." Judith turned on the bench and sat looking at him, still brushing. "Mackenzie told me a few details you left out, about the other night. . . . Hovik, what happens tomorrow if this thing doesn't work?"

"You mean, can Decker take over the country and all that?"

"No, we've already gone over that." She held her brush in her lap for a moment, letting her long unbraided hair fall loose about her face and shoulders. "I mean what happens to us, here."

Hovik blew out his breath and stared at the ceiling. "Most likely Decker goes on his way to Arizona or wherever and forgets about us. Or maybe he doesn't forget, but even if everything goes his way it'll be years before he can get around to coming after us. And whatever he does in the cities and the farm country, it'll be another story trying to take control of country like this. And," he said, "there's plenty of even wilder places in the mountains. Hell, even in the old days, when they had the whole country wired and everybody tagged and numbered, you could hide out in some parts of the northern Sierras or the Rockies for years."

He rolled on his side and pushed himself up on one elbow to face her. "And the kids will be big enough to travel pretty soon. So, yeah, we can still survive even if things get bad again."

She nodded, resuming her brushing. "That's what I thought. So why are we doing all this? Or rather," she said as he started to speak, "why are *you* doing it, getting involved again after all this time?"

He thought about it. "I guess," he said, "it's kind of to even things up."

She raised her eyebrows. He went on, "You know what happened the last time we did something like this. I thought," he said, forming his words slowly and with obvious difficulty, "if we do this and it keeps something bad from happening, keeps things from getting fucked up even worse, then maybe that would sort of even the score. A little, anyway."

She stood up, laying down her brush. "I'll be damned. Is this Franklin Roosevelt Hovik I'm hearing? Hey, don't look embarrassed, I'm impressed."

He lay back again, putting his hands behind his head. He said, "I told you I was getting old. Going soft."

She stood at the foot of the bed. "Really? Let's see about that."

She bent and undid his pants, tugging and jerking them off, hanging them over the bedpost, returning to finish undressing him, while he lay watching and grinning. "Good God, I don't care if this is the Long Night, this underwear has to go . . . raise your butt, Hovik, I've done enough heavy lifting for one day."

She stood beside the bed and dropped her cotton robe on the floor. Underneath she was naked. "You know what I miss, Hovik? Right now?"

"Pez candy?"

"Lingerie. I'd give nearly anything for, oh, a lace teddy and some nylons and a fancy garter belt. And some really trashy perfume . . . just once more, Hovik, I'd like to be a bimbo."

She climbed into bed and onto Hovik. "Now let's see. Oh, you're not getting old. Or soft, God knows," she said, fitting herself to him. "Not, ah, ah, not old at all."

Alice said to Mackenzie, "We really gotta talk, Mac."

He rolled over to face her, though he could not see her in the dark. "If you say so," he said. "Talk, I'm listening."

"Well—okay," she said, and then all in a rush, "I did it the other night, Mac. With, uh, with somebody. With a guy. At the forty-nine."

He waited. After a minute she said, "Well, damn, Mac, say something. Aren't you mad?"

"Do you want me to be?"

"Damn right. I want you to get really pissed off, tell me you'll kick my ass if I ever do it again. I'm tired of this don't-give-a-shit attitude of yours, Mac. I want somebody in the world to *care* what I do."

"All right," he said as she wiggled closer to him under the blanket. "All right, I care," he said, and realized suddenly that he did.

General Decker said, "Basic skills, Corporal Hooten. A soldier must never neglect basic skills. Consider those two spies who escaped the other night. This would not have happened if their hands had been tied properly."

"No sir," Hooten said.

"So this evening, Richie," Decker said, "I'm going to show you some really good ways to tie a man up. Valuable training, Richie, I hope you'll pay attention. Would you hand me those leather thongs, there's a good lad—"

15

Billy Blackhorse stood amid the rocks and cedars in the early light, listening to the groanings and bangings of the truck retreating back down the mountain road. When he could no longer hear it he turned and walked to the spot where the wires ended. He had already set the big orange-painted generator box beside the wires, getting a last lecture from Mackenzie as he did so; as instructed, he had not yet hooked up the wires to the terminals.

Now he slipped the small nylon backpack from his shoulders and laid it gently on the ground beside the exploder box and undid the top flap. It held such things as his binoculars, a thermos of hot soup, and a plastic bottle of water, but he ignored these for now.

Instead he reached deeper into the bag and, after a last quick glance around him, took out a small flat drum and a leather-wrapped beater stick.

Walking across the open rimrock, taking a stance at the cliff's edge and facing the rising sun, he held the drum in his left hand and began to tap a steady rhythm; and as the sun cut the eastern horizon he began to sing, softly at first and then more strongly, the song his grandfather had taught him.

On the other side of the canyon, standing on the highway shoulder overlooking the gorge and the railroad bridge, Joe Jack said, "How long you figure it'll be?"

"Awhile," Hovik said. "They won't come down that grade out of the high country very fast. They don't have that doodlebug to check out the track ahead and for all Decker knows we could of played hell with that track by now."

He took out his pack of cigarettes, saw that there were only four remaining, and put the pack back in his shirt pocket with a grimace. "Then," he said, "when they get to where we left the point buggy they'll stop and jack around with that awhile—I wish we'd thought to sabotage the engine that night—so all told, I'd say we got some waiting to do."

"Hm. So why'd we all get up early and come up here for sunrise services?"

Hovik grinned at him. "In case I'm completely full of shit."

"Good point," Joe Jack said seriously. He was looking across the canyon at the top of the cliffs. "I can't see Billy," he said.

"Long as he can see us," Hovik said. "When he has to."

"Uh huh . . . you know, Frank, I'm glad we're doing it this way. I mean, assuming it works and all." He turned and sat down on the highway guardrail, looking up at Hovik. "People like you and me, we're sort of career ass-kickers, you know? We tell ourselves all these stories about why we get into these things, but the truth is we do it because that's pretty much the way we are. If Decker hadn't come along we'd be picking a fight with somebody else before long."

He turned his head and looked out across the canyon again. "But these people—Billy, Alice, Larry, I guess all of them except Mackenzie—Jesus, Frank, guys like Decker eat people like them by the carload. Every damn one of them has been through some horrible shit in the last ten years, a lot of people like them across the country been through even worse, and somewhere in back of it there was always somebody like Decker that caused it."

Hovik nodded. "So?"

"Well, what I'm saying, all that stuff we did yesterday over there on the rimrock, and the rest of it—I just like it that they all got in on the operation, that's all. People like Decker," Joe Jack said, "been walking all over people like them for I guess a million years. I like it that they're getting a piece of him for a change."

The train sat on the spur track below the now-deserted mountain, its engines idling. Nothing moved in the entire scene except for a number of vultures and ravens that were beginning to circle and drop over on the far side of the mountain.

Standing on the steps that led up to the observation deck of his private car, General James Decker waited while the last two officers entered and joined the assembled group. Captain Grimshaw, he noticed, was looking a little disheveled. Understandable under the circumstances, but still. . . . He caught Grimshaw's eye and raised his eyebrows in a silent query. Grimshaw nodded, rather heavily. He looked depressed; his flushed face and clumsy movements suggested he had had a few drinks. Decker decided he would have to keep a close eye on Captain Grimshaw.

Decker cleared his throat. "Gentlemen," he said, "we are

about to embark on our historic journey. Before we depart, let us ask the blessings of our Supreme Commander on this enterprise."

They all bowed their heads. Decker raised his own to gaze up through the bulletproof glass of the observation dome.

"Almighty God," he began in a strong clear voice, "Who hath brought us to this place and this hour—"

The old pickup truck came whining and rattling up the hill and pulled off the road at the overlook. Hovik waved his hands urgently at Mackenzie, who was sitting behind the wheel. "Don't shut it off," he said. "Turn it around and get it headed downhill first. It was running okay yesterday but Christ, you can't ever be sure."

While Mackenzie got turned around Joe Jack said, "You used up just about all the good gas yesterday, didn't you?"

"Yeah, but I didn't dare take chances hauling that dynamite. We got enough left to run the bikes, but the truck's mostly running on alcohol now." He watched as Mackenzie stopped the truck next to the two parked motorcycles. "When this is over," he said, "let's go up and see if Decker left anything we can use. The way he talked, there was some good stuff he wasn't gonna have room for on the train." He made a face. "Of course it'd be just like the son of a bitch to destroy it all, just so nobody else can get it."

Mackenzie came walking across the highway, carrying a flat metal box. "All in place," he said. "Tom's up there watching the tracks, Larry and the others are set up down at the cut to take out the point buggy, and the others are over yonder in the woods, passing a joint and getting ready to watch the show."

"Passing a joint?" Hovik said.

"If you're gonna get blown away," Joe Jack observed, "might as well get blown away. . . ."

Standing under the observation dome, watching the trees and rocks slide past, Decker wondered suddenly how high they were. Altitude, he thought, might explain the sleeplessness and headaches that had bothered him lately, and perhaps the odd behavior of some of the men. It might be a factor worth figuring into his plans some day.

He unlatched the little folding metal map table from the wall. The maps were already clipped in place and he studied the elevation contour lines where they crossed the red line of the railroad. Six thousand feet or so, not as high as he'd thought. He raised his head and looked along the great swaying snake of the train. The engineer, he saw with satisfaction, was following orders and taking it easy on the long grade, using the brakes and at times the electrical drag of the enormous generators to slow the heavily loaded train.

Something suddenly struck him, a delayed recognition of something on the map. He looked again, farther down, along the main line.

"The bridge," he said aloud. "Of course. The bridge."

Mackenzie opened the metal box and took out the old brass flare pistol. "Christ," he said, breaking it open and looking down the barrel, "where'd you get this thing? The Yuba City Yacht Club?"

"Hey, you'd be surprised," Hovik told him. "They got a lot of big lakes up here in the mountains, where they dammed the rivers—hell, there's a dam on this river, farther down—and you had these people with boats and other people to sell stuff to them. We got that out of a place that also sold ski equipment."

Mackenzie fingered one of the fat cartridges. "Do you know if these flares actually work?"

"We never tried one," Joe Jack said. "But for God's sake don't try one now. Billy sees it, he'll hit that handle for all he's worth, train or no train."

"If it don't fire, we'll just fire a few shots in the air," Hovik added. "We already worked all that out."

"Hell of a time to bring this up," Joe Jack said, looking at the bridge, "but how do we know what part of the train we need to take out? I mean, I've seen that train, it's a good deal longer than that bridge. Any given point, there's gonna be at least a third of the whole train rolling along on solid land." He looked at Mackenzie. "Unless you found out what part he's got the nukes and stuff—"

"No sweat." Hovik pointed. "Look at that bridge, it ain't level. That train will still be going downhill all the way across—not much, it's a shallow grade, but any grade at all adds up to a hell of a lot of push with a loaded train. We knock out the front part, the cars in back will just slide on into the river after it."

"Can't the ones in back uncouple or something and hit their own brakes?"

Hovik shook his head. "They'll probably try, the poor bastards, but they won't have time. Christ," he said, "I'm glad I'm not on that train."

"You sound like you're starting to believe in this," Mackenzie remarked.

"Might as well," Hovik said. "It don't cost anything extra."

And after all, Mackenzie thought, why not? I've been to the Moon and I've seen the end of the world. Why should I have trouble believing anything else?

The train began to slow rapidly, with a great screech and hiss from underneath and a series of jerks that threw Decker off balance. He grabbed the handrail for support and peered out the windows in all directions, but there was nothing to see. The engines were out of sight, around a curve. He shouted, "Corporal Hooten!"

Before Hooten could respond a door opened and closed at the end of the car. A trooper appeared at the foot of the ladder, saluting. "General," he said, "they found the point buggy."

"Outstanding. Go back and pass the word, trooper, no one goes near it until we've checked it out. It could be boobytrapped. Corporal Hooten," he said, "find Sergeant Foley, have him reassemble his crew and then come see me. I've got some special instructions for him."

As the two men left Decker stared out the windows, thinking. Ought to order full defensive alert, this could be a trick to get them stopped, certainly plenty of cover here for an attack . . . but he didn't really believe it. It still had to be the bridge. If it happened, it would happen there.

Mackenzie said, "I'm not too happy about dropping a lot of nuclear material into a river. Eventually the containers will fail, even if they don't rupture on impact."

"Yeah, well," Hovik said, "there's always something. We'll quit fishing in this river, we'll pass the word to the people downstream—what few there are—and maybe some other stuff, I don't know. It's still better than having the damn things going off all over the country. Quit worrying so much."

Up on the mountainside overlooking the canyon, where the people from the camp were sitting under the trees, one of the women had started to sing an old country song about desperadoes waiting for a train. She was off key and she didn't really know the words, but nobody said anything. By now there was another joint going around and most of them thought she sounded pretty good.

The train rumbled through the last set of points and onto the main line, the sound of the wheels changing as they rolled onto the heavier rails and crossties. Picking up speed, it straightened itself into a long mottled column, the sun catching the great painted flags and eagles on the locomotives before they plunged into the shadow of the canyon.

Far ahead, moving much faster than the train now, the point buggy had already disappeared around the first bend, its engine blaring as the driver accelerated down the long straight stretch before the tracks made their big turn toward the river and the bridge.

Sitting cross-legged between the rails, Tom Crosses River closed his eyes and momentarily shut down everything but his hearing. He could do that; it was why they had given him this assignment. His hearing was legendary around the camp.

Now he nodded to himself, satisfied that he was right. Just to make sure, he laid his head on a rail. A faint distinct humming came from the steel.

Immediately he got to his feet, raised the twelve-gauge shotgun skyward, and fired, pumping the action and firing a second shot immediately, then waiting, counting to ten, before firing two more close-spaced shots.

Slinging the shotgun over his back, he ran to the nearby dirt road, straddled the small red trail bike that waited there, and kicked the starter hard. The engine caught on the third kick and Tom Crosses River clutched, shifted, and jammed hard down the road, back the way he had come, going fast as he dared, not about to miss this if he could help it.

Up on the rimrock, Billy Blackhorse heard the shots; the sound was distant and muffled but there was no mistaking the signal. Across the canyon somebody with a pistol—Hovik, probably—repeated the four-shot pattern, just to make sure, but Billy was already in motion.

Walking without haste, he followed the wires to their ends and sat down beside the exploder box. Carefully he fitted the bare ends of the wires to the terminals and screwed the brass terminals down tight. The handle of the plunge generator was already in position, all the way up.

His palms were sweating, but his mouth was very dry. He wiped his palms on his jeans. There seemed to be nothing he could do about his mouth. He stood, watching and waiting, wishing he could see what was happening in the canyon, wishing he could see something, wishing he knew whether he had time to pee.

On the highway Joe Jack said, "Like they say, she'll be coming around the mountain. Shouldn't take long now."

Mackenzie was sliding a flare cartridge into the breech of the old Very pistol. "I don't suppose they can see the truck and the bikes from the bridge," he said.

"Nah, we checked . . . damn, I can't hear anything that

sounds like a train, can you?" Hovik looked at Joe Jack. "You don't suppose Tom got hasty?"

But then a moment later they all heard the low-pitched drone of a decelerating diesel truck motor, and Mackenzie said, "The point buggy. Decker's sending the point buggy ahead to check out the bridge."

Almost immediately after he spoke they saw it, rolling slowly down the shallow grade where the railroad swung eastward to cross the river, coming to a stop a little way short of the bridge. They could hear the squeal of its wheels on the rails as it braked, the sound reaching them seconds after the point buggy stopped.

"Son of a bitch," Hovik said. "I knew it. They're gonna check that bridge out on foot. Decker probably figured this was where we'd do it."

The point buggy crew had already jumped down and deployed along the tracks, all but the man who remained on the fifty-caliber, covering them. Walking slowly, pausing here and there to examine a spot more closely, they moved out onto the bridge. One man even appeared to have a pair of binoculars to his eyes as he peered down at the girders and buttresses below his feet.

"Good thing we didn't try to blow the track," Joe Jack said. "No way in hell they wouldn't find the charges, see the wires, or something."

The men on the bridge were clearly engaged in something beyond a routine check. They moved with the deliberation of men who expect to find something and intend to take as long as necessary to find it. Now and then one or another lay down on the bridge and looked down between the ties or over the edge. Two men carried long rods with which they probed between ties and tapped at rail joints. "Jesus," Hovik said.

"The regular railroad inspectors probably didn't go over it that close back when it was being used."

"Listen," Mackenzie said.

From far up the canyon came a deep rumble, growing louder. "The train," Joe Jack said unnecessarily. "They better either hurry up or get ready to jump."

Hovik shook his head. "It's slowing down. That train ain't going near that bridge till those guys give the go-ahead."

"I never found out how they communicate," Mackenzie said absently, watching the men on the bridge. They were past the halfway point now. "Some kind of radio setup, I suppose off the truck battery or—"

"Train's stopped," Hovik said. They listened; it was true.

The men continued to pick their way across the bridge. The sun was high and it was getting hot.

Decker stood looking out through the observation dome, waiting. From where the train was stopped he had a fine view of the gorge, the great brown cliffs with their fanciful rock formations and the winding course of the river. He wondered why no one had built a dam here.

A door banged. Corporal Hooten came to the foot of the ladder. "Sir, the men report the bridge clear."

"Clear? What do you mean, clear?"

"They couldn't find anything, sir. No explosives, no signs of sabotage, nothing. Sergeant Foley says it's exactly as it was when they inspected it a few days ago, coming up here."

"What? You're sure that's what Foley said? That old radio set—"

"Sir, I made him repeat it twice. He was very positive."

"Well, I'm damned."

"You want me to tell him to look again, sir?"

"No, no, Richie, they've had long enough by now. And Foley's a good man, they're all hand-picked men, you know. No, if they found nothing there must be nothing. Strange." He looked out through the windows again, baffled. "Tell the engineer to carry on."

The point buggy sat on the far side of the bridge now, the men standing on the embankment beside it. Suddenly, evidently at an order, they all began climbing aboard. The buggy began to move slowly on down the track.

Joe Jack said, "I hope Larry and his boys remember not to go after those bastards until the dynamite goes off."

From back up the railroad, amplified by the walls of the canyon, came a loud shuddering rattle. The throbbing mutter of the idling diesels rose and changed into a great bass bellow.

Mackenzie said, "God, it's closer than I thought." He eared back the hammer of the flare pistol and pointed it skyward. "They won't be going very fast when they cross the bridge. I don't know if that's good or bad."

They saw it now, coming through the big cut on the west bank, the vivid colors of the painted flag on the lead engine making a startling splash in the shadowy canyon. As it moved out onto the spidery arch of the bridge Joe Jack said something in Cheyenne. It sounded like a prayer.

When the lead engine was just at the halfway point Mackenzie fired the flare pistol.

The flare burst high above the canyon, a sudden red flower in the pale hot sky. Billy Blackhorse bent over, wiped his hands once more on his jeans, grasped the wooden handle of the plunger with both hands, and, closing his eyes, slammed the handle down with all his weight and all his strength. The resistance was incredible; it felt as if the handle were barely moving at all. He knew with sick certainty that he had failed.

But then the whole world exploded in a blast so loud it numbed the senses. The shock wave nearly knocked him off his feet; the ground leaped violently underfoot, and he staggered and leaned on the generator handles to keep from falling.

He stood up, hearing bits of rock begin to fall all around him but paying no attention, even though some of the pieces were coming very close. He opened his eyes just in time to see the rock knob tilt gradually, almost lazily forward and disappear below the rim of the cliff.

Deaf, stunned, almost unbearably happy, Billy Blackhorse ran toward the cliff's edge to see what he had done.

Decker watched from his observation dome as the train rounded the curve and moved toward the bridge. He could see forward down the length of the train, clear to the square-backed shapes of the locomotives, and he watched them move out across the bridge with a sudden great surge of pride. God, he thought, to have a picture of this: the train soaring high above the gorge, its country's colors blazing, the towering cliffs above—

Then, as he glanced up at the cliffs, he saw a big puff of dust and smoke up near the rim; and, before he could fully grasp this, a large knob of rock detached itself and started to tumble downward. For an instant his mind was blank, but then suddenly his eyes registered the perspective and he saw that the thing was gigantic; and then he saw what was about to happen, and then he began to scream.

* * *

From the highway Mackenzie watched the great stone knob break free and begin to fall, turning as it rumbled down the cliff, end-over-end in a growing cloud of dust and stones. It seemed to move slowly at first, gathering momentum as it fell. The train, he saw without lowering his eyes, was well out onto the bridge now, the lead engine more than three-quarters of the way across and still moving.

The sound of the explosion reached them then, unexpectedly loud, echoing violently back and forth off the cliffs and rattling up and down the canyon. Through the last echoes came the distant faint squealing of steel wheels as someone, hopelessly, tried to put on the brakes.

The huge rock struck the protruding shoulder halfway down the cliff, bounced up and outward, hit the shoulder again, flipped almost lazily into the air, and soared out away from the cliff in a graceful parabola.

The kid was right, Joe Jack thought dazedly, it *is* damn near as big as a house.

From this distance the enormous rock appeared almost to float through the air toward the bridge, turning slowly on some invisible axis. A ray of sunlight, striking down a bend in the canyon, glanced briefly off a blasted corner of stone. The trajectory was almost vertical now, the great mass gathering speed as it plummeted into the gorge.

It's going to miss, Mackenzie thought. It's too low, it's short.

To some of the observers it seemed at first that the rock did miss, passing close on the far side of the train and the bridge. To Billy Blackhorse, viewing the scene from high above, it appeared that the rock merely glanced lightly off the side of the lead locomotive and then the edge of the bridge, a minor grazing blow incapable of doing any real harm.

Hovik said, "Christ. Did it—"

Then they all saw the lead engine tilt violently to one side, tipping crazily, a toy locomotive suddenly kicked by a petulant child. The second locomotive was beginning to move strangely too, its leading end being dragged sideways by the toppling engine ahead, its wheels screaming on the rails and then gradually, irresistibly, breaking free of the tracks.

The monster rock smashed into the side of the lead engine with great and terrible force, crushing the metal in the middle of the painted flag, slapping the heavy locomotive almost casually off the track; then, its energy unchecked, it rapped a jagged corner against the bridge itself, instantly wrecking a section of rail, before tumbling on into the gorge and smashing into the river.

The shock ran back along the train, throwing men off their feet. On his observation platform Decker clutched the railing for support, staring forward along the train. As he watched, the two locomotives, still coupled together, slid slowly off the bridge. He felt the sudden acceleration under his feet as the weight of the engines pulled the train forward, and then the train's own momentum took over as the engines broke free, the long string of heavily loaded cars driving relentlessly forward and derailing and falling, one by one and in strings, and he screamed, the horrible drawn-out howl of an animal gone mad, as the deck tilted sharply under his feet and he saw, through the bulletproof glass pressed against his face, the waiting river below.

From the distant mountainside and the high cliffs there was something bizarre, almost comic, in the spectacle: the tiny, brightly painted locomotives plunging madly off the bridge, dragging half a dozen cars after them, to splash into the river with great fountains of water. Behind them, wheels screeching, couplings clanging, more toy cars rolled with ridiculous inevitability onto the bridge and lurched over the side and fell helter-skelter into the river or onto the rocks. Only the nearest watchers were able to hear, faint and terrible through the steel din, the sound of hundreds of human voices screaming.

On the mountainside, on the highway, at the cliff's edge, everyone stood and watched as the armored train of the Army of America plunged to its death in the depths of the gorge.

VIETNAM FICTION
by Cat Branigan

An authentic new series on the Vietnam air war, in the tradition of Worldwide's successful VIETNAM: GROUND ZERO.

- __ **WINGS OVER NAM #1: Chopper Pilot**
  A20-800 ($3.95, USA) ($4.95, CAN)
- __ **WINGS OVER NAM #2: The Wild Weasels**
  A20-802 ($3.95, USA) ($4.95, CAN)
- __ **WINGS OVER NAM #3: Linebacker**
  A20-805 ($3.95, USA) ($4.95, CAN)
- __ **WINGS OVER NAM #4: Carrier War**
  A20-806 ($4.95, USA) ($5.95, CAN)
- __ **WINGS OVER NAM #5: Bird Dog**
  A20-808 ($4.95, USA) ($5.95, CAN)

Warner Books P.O. Box 690
New York, NY 10019

POPULAR LIBRARY

Please send me the books I have checked. I enclose a check or money order (not cash), plus 95¢ per order and 95¢ per copy to cover postage and handling,* or bill my ☐ American Express ☐ VISA ☐ MasterCard. (Allow 4-6 weeks for delivery.)

___Please send me your free mail order catalog. (If ordering only the catalog, include a large self-addressed, stamped envelope.)

Card # _____

Signature _____ Exp. Date _____

Name _____

Address _____

City _____ State _____ Zip _____

*New York and California residents add applicable sales tax.

471